UNDER

Book Two of Luna's Story

DIANA KNIGHTLEY

Other titles by Diana Knightley can be found here:

Leveling: Book One of Luna's Story

Under: Book Two of Luna's Story

Deep: Book Three of Luna's Story

DianaKnightley.com

For Isobel, Fiona, Gwyneth, and Ean
Please, always, roll the wagon back up the hill,
your friends will help.

Part One:

The Storm

Chapter 1

"Hi," Luna's voice emitted from the radio.

"Long day?"

"Yes, but the weather was good, the wind at our backs. We made it to camp and now we're eating."

"How many people are there?"

"Over twenty—" Her voice broke and Beckett lost track until, "— not sure yet."

"I'm sorry I lost you, what aren't you sure of?"

"Who's coming to the mainland with me."

"They might not go? What will they do?"

"Adapt. But don't worry, I'll come."

"But…"

"It'll be okay Beckett. I'll see you in two weeks right? That's what you need to focus on. Where are you headed?"

"North. Away. The opposite direction." Beckett exhaled a deep breath. "I can't wait to see you, really see you. The next two weeks are going to be long."

"Did the doctor look at your hands, are you okay?"

"Yes, I'm okay, the dip this morning didn't hurt me. At least not physically. My reputation around here may have taken a hit."

"Speaking of your reputation, everyone here wants to say hello."

A loud chorus, "Hi, Beckett!" erupted from the speaker.

"Tell them hello, tell them if they go with you to the mainland, we can meet for real."

Luna giggled. "That might convince Sky. She's seen enough of you to follow you anywhere. All she talks about is your ass. Right, Sky?"

Sky said, "Were you saying something Luna? I was thinking about Beckett's ass."

Beckett groaned.

Luna giggled, "But me most of all. It really was a nice departing gesture. I'll have motivation on my paddle."

Beckett chuckled. "Well, if it gets you to paddle faster, I'm glad I exposed myself to everyone today."

"I'll paddle fast enough."

"I'm glad you're safe. I'm glad I found you. I still can't believe it."

"Me neither, but you did, and like you said, it means something all that finding. I have to go, Beckett. We have a lot to talk about the group and I and . . . I'll talk to you tomorrow."

"You'll leave in the morning? I need your coordinates. Where do you think you'll end up?"

"I don't know what time I'll leave yet, or where I'll land. It looks like we'll have rain tonight. We'll weather it here in camp and then I'll take off, after it's over."

"But we'll talk tomorrow, right?"

"At sunset, or 7:30 your time."

"Okay, I love you Luna."

"I love you too."

The radio went silent.

Beckett stared at it, still, quiet, dead.

It was great to be able to talk to Luna, to know she was okay. It also sucked, to talk to Luna from this far away.

———————

The next night at 7:15, Beckett entered the galley, assembled the charts and the radio, and took a deep breath. Before he could begin though, Dan, followed by Sarah, Rebecca, and Jeffrey, clamored down the steps. Dan and Sarah slid into the seat opposite him, Rebecca shoved him with her hip to give her a place to sit beside him. Jeffrey leaned over the back of the adjoining booth.

Beckett said, and hoped it didn't sound as surly as he thought it did, "I might want to do this alone."

Rebecca said, "Sure, but this is Luna, paddling on her own, and we're all going to wait here with you until we know. Then we'll go."

Beckett took another big breath and turned the radio on.

He adjusted the dial for their most recent channel and asked, "Luna? Luna Saturniddae?"

Static greeted him. He twisted the dial and repeated, "Luna?"

Emerging from the static, faintly, "Beckett?"

Everyone in the galley cheered and then quieted.

Beckett adjusted the volume, such relief in his heart. "Luna, I'm here, Luna are you good?"

Her faint, barely heard response, "Yeah. I'm good . . . paddled all day with a bright sun overhead . . . . . . have excellent weather until midweek—"

Beckett couldn't hear the end of the sentence over the cheering and clapping of Dan, Sarah, and Jeffrey. Rebecca hugged him around the shoulders.

Beckett said, "That's great Luna, really great, I was so — that's great. The crew here wants to say hello!"

Luna's voice called, "Hi Beckett's friends!"

They all joyously yelled hello and goodbye and raucously clambered to the deck leaving Beckett alone.

He said, "First give me your coordinates."

He marked them on the charts but before he could finish she said, "There's a good wind behind me. I plan to get to the Central Bank Outpost tomorrow. I have to sleep in the open tonight, but the wind will be calm."

"Can we talk in the morning? I — today wasn't easy."

"Yeah, nine o'clock sharp, we'll talk, tomorrow."

"Okay, thanks. Was it hard saying goodbye to Sky?"

"Very hard. They didn't understand why I was leaving. They tried to talk me out of it, but . . . her family paddled with me for a bit singing a song of goodbye . . ." Luna continued to talk but Beckett could barely hear over the flood of relief. She was alive, in motion, meeting him.

He said, "When we get to shore we'll get you signed in at the camps and I'll get you signed out and . . ." His voice trailed off remembering all the things he needed to handle when he returned to shore. There was a lot. He didn't want to tell Luna about all the things he had left undone.

She said, "I'm thinking about resting at the outer Shield Island for a day or two, if the weather is good. It has amenities and is within a day's paddle of the port. That way we can arrive at the same time."

"I'd like that. I'll go with you to register. That would be good."

"Here's what you have to understand, I've got this. This isn't anything to fear, it's simply something to get through."

"Yes, but . . ."

"Tell me something cool about your house, Beckett."

"We have gardens all around, and my Aunt Dilly put up bird houses and feeders everywhere. They're all painted bright colors; it looks like crazy people live there, but it's really beautiful."

"It does sound beautiful; I can't wait to see it. How will we get to your house from Heighton Port?"

"Um, good question." Beckett's fingers were gripping and rubbing on his scalp. "I have my motorcycle, but your paddleboard won't fit — I'll figure it out. I could rent a truck or something."

Luna's faint faraway voice said, "I need to go. I have farther to paddle and then batten down the hatches, except I don't own hatches."

"Goodnight Luna, I miss you."

"Goodnight Beckett. I miss you too."

Chapter 2

Luna paddled. Her eyes locked on the horizon, one thought on her mind. The finish line looming. Two weeks.

She had one aim, Heighton Port. There, the worst of this experience, this trip, this ordeal, would be behind her. The aching muscles, the blisters, the gnawing fear, the desperate loneliness — would be over. Two weeks. For good.

But also, this was everything she had known for so long. Days and days of ordeal.

There had been a short respite with Sky and her group, but that had been preceded by mega trauma and ordeal. A flash of a moment with Beckett. But, oh, the weeks before Beckett had been awful. The kind of weeks someone shouldn't have to live through. Lonely, desperate, sad.

It was awful being alone, and she did not want to do it anymore.

This whole thing, this big paddle across the ocean, was all because Beckett had promised that she would never be alone again. If not those exact words, it was what he meant, and she believed him. Beckett meant she had someone.

She meant it too.

But she was scared.

She had been telling Beckett that she wasn't afraid. That there was nothing to fear, but she hadn't been completely truthful. She was terrified. Just of a different thing.

Beckett was scared of losing her. That he wouldn't find her again. That she would become lost and never found.

His fear was close to being over.

That was good, she was happy for him.

Her fear was entirely different.

She was headlong rushing into a life that was absolutely different.

She had no idea what to expect and didn't know if she would like it.

Her whole life, her family, had scoffed at the idea of living on land. To Waterfolk there wasn't an in-between, you were either — or. Waterfolk or a boring Stiffneck. No one in her acquaintance had ever been both.

Meeting Beckett at a dock, signing in at a camp, riding on his motorcycle to his mountain, living in his house. These things were taking her away from her life, her identity, her essence.

Luna had been truthful (sort of) when she said she wasn't afraid of becoming lost. She hadn't been fully honest. She was terrified of being found.

But she loved Beckett.

That much was enough to paddle closer and closer to his shore.

Chapter 3

On the fifth day Beckett began their conversation with, "You good?"

"It was a long day. I paddled against the wind for most of it, trying to beat a southern storm to Otter Island." Her voice broke up.

Beckett scanned the maps. "Did you say Otter Island or Outer Island?"

Luna kept talking, ". . . cut north for shelter . . . . . . an inlet . . . lay low . . ."

Beckett traced his pencil up and around the islands along the northern coast of the mainland, searching for any that matched her words. But his charts rarely matched her descriptions. He asked, "What are the coordinates?"

She rattled off numbers, but her voice broke. He asked again, she repeated them, with static through most of it. He asked a third time and marked the closest thing he could decipher.

She was somewhere inside a chain called the Sierra Islands. A location that caused Dan to go, "Wow, those islands are notorious for their insane weather, tell her to go fast."

Well, she wasn't going fast. Her mark had barely moved from yesterday's. Here, Beckett was on a boat with a crew of people caring for his health and wellbeing, and what did Luna have?

Nothing. She was on her own, crossing the ocean. The rising ocean.

"I wish you had someone with you."

"I couldn't let Sky . . . . . . offered to but I couldn't let them. To separate them from their group . . . . . . that's their family. You . . ." Her voice trailed off.

Beckett, head in his hand, asked, "What?"

"Waterfolk can't make it without their family."

Beckett gulped. "Luna I'm sorry you have to. You found a family and now I made you leave them. And you're alone again and if anything happens to you —"

". . . static . . . didn't mean it to make you feel guilty, I just . . . . . . somehow I am surviving . . . . . . glad when I don't have to anymore."

"Me too. I admire you that you're so strong and brave."

"I don't feel strong . . . . . . this isn't bravery, most of the time I'm kind of terrified . . . . . . I'm really tired . . . . . . Mr. Wind and I need to have a talk about his timing."

"God, Luna I'm so sorry."

"What I need right now . . . distractions . . . . . . grateful for this radio."

"Describe where you are."

" . . . . . . inlet . . . a canopy of trees. The shore has some boulders. I pulled Steve and Boosy and Tree up out of the water and tied them . . . my tent . . . . . . higher ground. I can look out the door . . . " There was a zipping sound. "I can see Tree, he looks good, which means Boosy and Steve are good."

"What time did the storm start?"

"It started raining . . . . . . half hour ago . . . direction and size of the front . . . it will last all night."

Beckett was drawing a spiral around her possible co-ordinates, darker and darker. "I thought you would be closer by now."

There wasn't any reply for a moment until Luna's voice emerged, ". . . the weather and I'm alone," faintly, "I wonder if—"

A roaring sound interrupted her. Beckett sat up and leaned in. "Is that the rain?"

There was no response until, ". . . I should go."

The radio went dead.

"Luna, are you okay?"

Beckett stared at for a long moment, then he studied the charts, tracing a line from her coordinates, to his own, miles and leagues away.

Chapter 4

The next morning the H2OPE anchored off a small outer island. Little more than sandy beaches and a rocky interior, with a few scrub trees clutching rocky outcrops. Thousands of birds flocked on every surface of water and land.

Beckett leaned on his favorite deck railing while birds swooped and flapped above the boat.

Dan stalked up. "Watch your head these look like poopers." Bird poop splattered the deck beside Beckett's foot. Dan laughed and called to Jeffrey, "Good news! Beckett's hands have healed enough, he'll be able to help swab the decks tonight."

Jeffrey said, "Good, because this is one big mess already and we've only been here for ten minutes." They all looked down, there was bird poop everywhere.

Rebecca pointed toward shore. "Turtles, see that? Turtles!"

Beckett peered in the direction she pointed. He couldn't see anything different from seagulls, pelicans, pipers. Rebecca grabbed a net and buckets and raced toward the awaiting Zodiac.

Dan said, "I better hustle to captain their boat."

Sarah ran by with more buckets, "Dan, hurry, turtles!"

Beckett's job was to remain on deck and receive the samples and return by pulley the empty buckets to be filled again. The crew fanned out across the sand, bent over, scanning, collecting, digging, dragging bags and nets behind them as they travelled back and forth to the Zodiac.

Dan was sending two buckets of samples up by pulley. "You good up there Army?"

"How come Army is here on a ship while the ship's crew is on land?"

Dan flicked his wet hair. He didn't need to leave the Zodiac, but kept jumping out of it to plow waist deep through the water to collect the samples from the beachcombers. To a stranger it would have seemed selfless that he kept everyone else from getting wet, but the crew and Beckett knew Dan did it because he loved the water. Had to be in it.

Dan said, "You're not in the water though are you? Always looking for any excuse to stay dry on higher ground."

Higher ground. That was one of the last things Luna said, she was on higher ground. Now it had been hours and hours since their call was cut off…

Beckett unclasped the buckets, lugged them to the lab, poured them into tanks, and sent the empty buckets down the line back to Dan. Beckett said, "Better the high ground than the low, that's where you have to swim."

Dan laughed, ""Do you even know how to swim Army? Maybe we could get you some of those inflatable armband floaty things." He sped the Zodiac in a wide circle to the beach.

———————————

Hours later everyone returned to the ship. The day had been a tremendous success. They had found about ten sea turtle nests, a sure sign that they were thriving, even with the hungry birds overhead. Sarah had some wild theories about how the one could live in harmony with the other, but said, "These are all conjectures though, I'll need to study this, really study it." They had taken photographs, notes, and recordings, and with the specimens and samples would have more than enough to catalog and study. For months.

Rebecca said, "We have to celebrate before Sarah and I disappear to start our research, let's meet in the galley at sunset so we can par-ty!"

Beckett and Jeffrey grabbed mops and began the work of scrubbing the decks while everyone else set about doing the sunset work of the ship.

After dinner, Dan emerged from the kitchen with a tray of shot glasses and poured drinks and passed them around, but Beckett shook his head. "Nah man, don't drink."

"Even to celebrate?"

Beckett said, "Nope."

Dan paused for a second eyes squinted.

Beckett asked, "What?"

"Never met any army guy that didn't drink, escapism is the entire point, or didn't you know?"

"Just not my point." Beckett looked away.

Dan said, "Sure, of course, no offense meant." He continued handing drinks to everyone else.

Captain Aria asked, "Sarah, perhaps you'd like to say a few words?"

Sarah stood, raised her glass, and cleared her throat. "Mark your history books people. Rebecca and I have, on this day, found thriving turtle nests. We also spotted an endangered seabird that we thought was long gone. The water quality around the island was excellent. So much flora and fauna there. Fish. Crabs. Shells. It was amazing."

Everyone cheered their glasses and Dan said, "To baby turtles, and their cute little legs!"

Rebecca said, "We'll stay tomorrow and then we head back to port, this has been an excellent trip. Nothing but good news."

Dan said, "Except of course Army's hands."

Beckett chuckled. "Hear hear."

———————

After dinner as the crew went singing to the upper decks, Beckett attempted to radio Luna.

"Hello Luna, are you there?"

— static —

"Luna?"

— static —

He fiddled the dial back and forth repeating her name. All he heard were the usual voices, conversations, and one faint voice, garbled and masculine. Finally he gave up.

———————

Beckett leaned on his favorite portion of railing, looking over the darkened ocean. The ship was facing west. The island they were anchored beside was northwest. Beckett faced east, thinking about the distance between where he stood, Luna, and land.

Snippets of the crew's revelry reached his ears. Jeffrey and Rebecca were singing a drunken song. "With a howeeeeee yo!"

Beckett chuckled, they were seriously out of tune.

Behind him Sarah, usually quiet and sensible, squealed and giggled, "Whoa, Tiger."

Dan laughed merrily. "I can't help myself you're so hot, Baby."

Rebecca yelled, "Get a room!" and everyone laughed.

The water below where he stood was deep and black as night. The sky above was cloudy and grey and low. Like the up and down were reversed. The sea seemed endless, the sky close. And it was really. They were all moving higher as the sea grew.

Sarah thought this island was nothing but good news. But she had been looking at it from the surface — the water's edge was thriving. From Beckett's perspective though, up above, from the boat deck — the same perspective he had from his Outpost, the same as from his mountain home, looking down at what was happening — it was clear.

The sea was rising. Pushing everything (and everybody) up and up to the last available spaces, where they were clawing and clamoring for purchase on the last remaining ground.

Maybe before there were twenty islands with three sea turtle nests on each one. Now there were three islands, with five sea turtle nests. He wanted to be happy, to celebrate with them, but he couldn't. He could only mourn the loss of all that land.

He usually looked up at night, but tonight's cloudy, starless sky gave him one less thing to worry about. If it had been a star-filled sky, Beckett would feel very small.

He didn't want to feel small. He wanted to feel in control, able to do this.

Instead he had that anxious, skin crawling, dread, like any news coming his way wasn't going to be good.

He tried to tell himself that his worries were always wrong. He had worried that the Outpost would collapse below him. It didn't. That Luna was dead. She wasn't. That he wouldn't find her. And guess what, in the entire ocean, he found her.

It would be impossible to lose her now. The fates didn't have that kind of humor.

His luck would hold.

Or maybe it wouldn't.

He gripped the railing, took a deep, head-down breath, blew it out and straightened.

He walked over to the others. Jeffrey and Dr Mags were lounging on deckchairs. Rebecca held a bottle, loosely, by its neck, and slurred, "In the expanthe of the univerth I saw a turtle nest and that was awesome," before she lost track of what she wanted to say and giggled.

Dan's face was buried in Sarah's shoulder, whispering in her ear.

Beckett interrupted, "I'm headed to bed." He tried for an upbeat, merry tone.

The others called, "G'night Beckett!"

And he headed to his bunk to sleep.

Chapter 5

Luna stared at the underside of her tent roof listening to the pounding rain. Or not really listening, more like living through. It was so brain-numbingly loud, terrifying, blood chilling, cry-inducingly loud, and it had been raining since yesterday. Hours. Hours and hours and hours.

So she tried to Go Bird. Like her mom had told her when she was little, *Go bird little Luna*.

Her mother had said that birds lived joyful lives, but they had to live through terrible weather sometimes — just like Waterfolk. To get through, birds folded their wings around like a hug and hunkered down. And they weren't scared. Birds weren't anything, because they turned off their 'what ifs' and went completely still and quiet. The whole time. Blank.

Then, after the storm had passed, those birds flew again, joyous and energetic. Because they could turn off their 'what ifs.' That was key.

So Luna tried to Go Bird, but the problem was, there weren't any other birds on her branch. She couldn't turn her brain off because she was in charge of her own survival. When she was little, she could Go Bird because her father and mother were in charge of her safety. Not now. Not anymore. And that sucked.

Crack!

Her heart raced. What the hell was that? Something above her tent (tree branch, tree, rock?) was cracking. It would crash down.

She curled up into a ball and huddled, hard.

Her breaths were ragged and gasping.

WHOOSH, a terrifying falling of something crashing close. A scraping on the fabric of her tent. The deafening rain.

She huddled harder. No pain though. No pain. No pain.

She opened her eyes. The tent roof was an inch away from her face. Outside roared.

She shoved up on the roof, crawled from under it, and unzipped the door. Water rushed all around, over, under, and through. A raging river had formed and she was in the middle of it. She checked the tent corners. Her tent stakes were barely holding on, pulling up from the mud, releasing their grasp.

"Shit shit shit." She withdrew and held up the roof, while she frantically wadded up her bedding and stuffed it into a sack, counting one, two, three, four — forcing herself — faster, faster.

Because her best guess was, *three minutes.*

She leapt from the tent into the muck and water — ankle deep. Below: the hill had rushed away in a slide. She yanked a front stake. The tent pulled furiously. She twisted up the other front stake, the tent slid to the right. She waded upstream through the rushing water to the back end of the tent, and dislodged another stake — the tent pitched and spun, fast, down and away fast. Luna dove after it frantically trying to grab the last corner of LITERALLY EVERYTHING she owned in the world. "Crapitycrapcrap." She caught it.

She clutched the tent in her fist.

But it didn't want to stay in her fist, stupid tent. It struggled with all the power of gravity, weight, force, and dramatic natural storm surge toward — Away. Like a jerk, a bona fide jerk. It wanted to leave her. Alone on this stupid island with rain pouring down. Alone without anything.

Luna dug her heels in, gathered the tent, hauled it up on her body, scream-begging the universe to help her keep her stuff, wondering — *what kind of idiot takes the stakes out of a tent in a raging river with everything they owned inside?* If her brothers had been here, they would have called her a Stink Crawler because that's what they called everyone too asinine to know how to survive on water. Stink Crawler. She deserved the name. Her brothers wouldn't have been surprised. This was exactly the kind of thing she did. Not thinking shit through.

She dug her heels in deeper and pulled and pulled, heaving with all her strength. Rain pouring down, visibility at — freaking zero. Maybe a foot if she wanted to open her eyes. She didn't. Holding everything across her body, she reached over and twisted up the last stake in the final corner.

The tent yanked downward, causing her to lose her footing and slide for ten feet, like a boat, a slippery, sliding, perfectly dynamic, floating watercraft. Her tent wanted down in a torrential slip-slide river of mud and water. And it wanted out to sea.

Leaving her. Just. Like. Everyone. Else.

But Luna's hand, without any conscious thought, scrambled and caught a branch. She strained, screaming from the effort, digging her feet under her, keeping the tent, she dragged and pulled, slipping and struggling, until finally, gratefully, her feet found firm ground on the river's bank.

Luna dropped to her knees, let go of the branch, but then slid down the river bank, the weight of the tent dragging her down through brambles and branches. Did it enjoy her desperation? Was it mocking her?

Finally she slammed into a tree trunk and held on. She fought against the slippery downward pull of the torrential down rush, gathering, heaving, straining, until she had the bulk of the tent and LITERALLY EVERYTHING she owned safely on the fern-covered bank, not rushing away.

She dropped back in the pouring rain and muck and mud and yelled, "AAAARRRRGGGGGGH."

And then only after the ordeal did she begin to sob. Tears rolled down her face mixing with the rain and matching the river rushing by her feet. She cried because that sucked, because she almost died, but also and mostly, because she wasn't dead yet. It was going to happen. Death was just toying with her first.

She wiped her streaming eyes with her sodden wrist, sat up and clutched her knees, head down, and tried to calm herself.

She took stock: This area looked like it wouldn't rush away, but the last place seemed safe three hours ago. She couldn't trust these ferns and trees to protect her. And the rain was unrelenting. A rain like this would last for days.

She held onto a corner of the tent, refusing to let go, while she scanned the hillside. Visibility sucked. The only way to survive was up. She hoisted the tent's corner to her shoulder and dragged it, and LITERALLY EVERYTHING she owned inside, through the underbrush. It caught on roots and twigs until she stumbled to a spot that would work for what she needed — collapse. Despair. Dramatic despondence and dismay.

She staked the bottom down, arranged the tent poles (one bent awkwardly, so the roof caved in) and attempted to stretch the loops and panels over the poles — the fucking last hook wouldn't hook on the final — she dropped it, banged her feet up and down, and screamed at the sky. This was so freaking frustrating she needed to — she gulped a deep breath, picked up the hook, and forced it around the pole.

And dove into the tent.

She was sopping, drenched, wet to her core.

The tent was wrecked.

The roof bowed down filling with water. If a pool collected, it would begin to seep in. She knocked it upward and it immediately filled again. Great. There would be no sleeping tonight.

The rain was relentless, the sound terrifying. And that — that river, that catastrophe, that near death experience — had been really close. Too close.

She drew her knees to her chest and wrapped her arms around and cried. The rain didn't let up for twenty more hours.

Chapter 6

Beckett slept soundly but woke with a start. He looked around at the hulking bodies asleep in all the other bunks.

What time was it? It was still very dark, but the bunk room had tiny round sand-blasted windows. He crept to the bathroom and checked the wall clock, thinking about his watch, on Luna's arm — somewhere.

He hadn't spoken to Luna in thirty-four hours.

It was early morning yet and everyone else had partied really hard last night.

He crept to the deck and entered the galley, unrolled the charts and got out the radio.

Turning the dial, he listened. Static, static, nothing but static. "Luna? Luna Saturniddae? Anna Barlow? Luna?" He repeated the questions at all the usual channels and then randomly, hand on his head, twisting the dial, going around again.

She wasn't expecting to talk to him now. They had agreed to talk in the evening. Every night. But last night she hadn't answered, and his anxious feeling was growing. And growing.

He hoped that waking early might mean magic would happen — he would say, "Luna," into the radio, and she would be magically answer. Magic would be good right about now.

He sighed.

A hand clapped on his back. Dan said, "You're up before me, Army?"

Beckett nodded. "Yeah, just—"

"When was the last time?" Dan slid into the booth.

"Night before last. She was in a storm."

Dan exhaled. "Phew man, that sucks."

"Yes. It does. I was checking to see if she—"

"Sure. That makes sense. I'm going to put the coffee on, the troops will be up in a minute, and they'll need it after last night."

He rose from his seat then paused. "She's okay, she'll answer tonight."

Beckett nodded. Even though he wondered, *would she?*

Dan watched his face and repeated, "She will." He left for the kitchen. Beckett turned the radio off and rolled up the charts.

Dan returned with a mug of coffee for Beckett, spinning it so the handle pointed away because Beckett's bandaged hands would hold the cup easier without it. He said, "Also wondering why Army doesn't drink."

Beckett said, "My uncle drank enough for everyone."

"Ah see, we're starting to get to know each other," Dan returned to the kitchen to begin cooking as Jeffrey entered the galley followed by everyone else.

Chapter 7

Beckett stood, not really thinking about what he would do next, grabbed the charts, and climbed to the bridge and knocked.

Lenny answered and gestured him through to Captain Aria.

"Yes, Beckett?" She jotted into a notebook then closed it and stashed it away on a shelf.

Beckett glanced around the bridge. this was his first time there. He was unsure whether the large amount of buttons and screens, flashing lights and beeping noises made him feel more comfortable or not. It was a little unnerving that so much information was necessary for this ship's safe passage. *I hope Captain Aria knows what she's doing.* He gulped and drew his attention back to Captain Aria who was waiting with her brows up, incredulous, like she knew what he was thinking.

"Yes, um Captain, can I speak with you?"

She said curtly, "You are." Why was it that every interaction with her seemed to turn him into a complete ass? It would be better if he had a plan, but no, he jumped without thinking. Every conversation. And they mattered.

"I just got off the radio — Luna, um, the young woman?" He shifted his feet. "And thank you for the radio again."

Captain Aria said, "Your point please?"

"Oh yes, um, she's missing."

Captain Aria squinted her eyes. "Missing for how long?"

Beckett drew air before saying, "Thirty-seven hours. She's in a storm, by herself, the radio cut out, and now there's been no contact." He hoped she would consider that long enough to be concerned.

Captain Aria leveled her gaze and stared at him imperiously. "For thirty-seven hours."

He met it. "Yes." He tried for confident and worried, both, in turns.

"How often did you speak before?" Her hands went to her hips.

"Except for the first day, every twenty-four, without fail. Sometimes more often."

Captain Aria nodded. "John, Lenny, will you please look over the charts with Beckett? You have her latest coordinates?"

"Yes," Beckett unfurled the charts on the map table. He pointed to Luna's final coordinates, circled, with dark pencil, around and around. That looked a little desperate. But he hadn't thought to erase it — hadn't thought. Why was he like this, acting without thinking? Like an animal. A cornered animal.

John and Lenny conferred. They agreed that she was probably near the outer edge of the Sierra Islands. They asked Captain Aria about the weather. She said, "That whole area is under Severe Weather Advisory Sierra Squall season. I can see the bank of clouds from here. It's not particularly safe on a boat, but alone on a…" Her voice drifted off. She returned to sitting in her high seat, in front of the wheel, and looked out the bridge window at the horizon.

Lenny said, "Would take us about six hours to get close enough."

Beckett's head snapped up. Were they actually discussing going? He hadn't considered it a possibility. He hoped. But actually going had seemed a long shot.

Captain Aria said, "I will give you the chance to ask Rebecca, Sarah, and the group. If they are finished with the bulk of their research and willing to go out of the way, we'll discuss the change of course."

Beckett said, "Oh my — thank —" Her hand shot up, stopping him mid sentence.

"I'm not saying yes. Ask the researchers, they get to make the final decision."

Beckett said, "Okay, definitely." He made to roll up the charts, but Captain Aria stopped him.

"We'll need those. Leave them."

Beckett made an awkward half-bow out of the room and jogged to the galley.

"Rebecca! Sarah!"

Chapter 8

Luna lay curled around her knees, staring at her arm, at the band of the watch, dazed. How long had she been here? For too many long uncountable hours. She sent the pooled water away with a splash. It filled immediately.

Her ears hurt from the deafening noise, and now her whole head hurt. like it was squeezed, pressure, noise, ache, stress. Her jaw was constantly clenched. She was shivering cold. Her skin hurt because of the wet-cold-clammy everything.

How many hours? She shifted her arm to allow herself a glimpse of Beckett's grandfather's watch. It didn't help. Time had passed, too much and too little, an endless loop of night and day — and she had thought herself found, but no.

She was lost.

She kept thinking about what her brothers would say: she was an idiot. A dying alone, idiot. A couldn't do anything right, not even the most basic things, deserved what happened to her — because what kind of person ends up like this, alone, terrified, lost, making these kinds of mistakes? Life and death. Bad knots, poor directions, unsafe tent positions. These weren't just mistakes. These were the kind of things that caused calamity. People could die. Would. Did. And she was a navigator. A part of a nomad family. A paddler. And she was going to die lost, alone, on land. A storm raining down.

A never-ending storm.

Because of never ending mistakes. Bad knots.

And she thought she was going to live with Beckett on a mountainside. Happy.

God, she was an idiot.

She couldn't even cry anymore, her head hurt too bad, her insides dried and withered, in opposition to her sopping wet outsides.

She wrapped around Beckett's watch and really did Go Bird. Past thinking, past hoping, past surviving.

Chapter 9

He had interrupted the hung-over munching and commiserating of the group as they swigged coffee and amicably bickered over who drank most and who suffered it more. Dan seemed to win with most. Rebecca felt it a lot. She held a wet compress to her head moaning when Beckett yelled her name.

Sarah said, "Shhhh, Beckett, we're right here."

Beckett slid into the booth beside Jeffrey across from Rebecca. "I have a thing to ask. I—"

Rebecca groaned and dropped her head down on an arm. "I can't think right now Beckett; can't we sit here quietly and not talk?" She closed her eyes and pretended to sleep.

"Not really, I don't have time."

She slid to an upright position.

Dan grabbed the coffee pitcher and refilled mugs. "From the look on Army's face we're going to need the caffeine." He sloshed the pitcher back to the counter and slid beside Sarah who immediately draped her head and arm across his shoulders, lazily.

Beckett looked around at the group, hung-over, tired, barely knew him, busy researching, and he was going to ask them to aim their ship in a different direction. To sail into a storm. He swigged coffee. "Luna is gone. I believe she's in trouble."

Rebecca lifted her head.

"I have her coordinates, but there's a big storm, and she's in it alone. I spoke to Captain Aria about it. It would take us six hours to get there. But I need you all to agree." Beckett's bandaged hands were out in front. He hurriedly put them under the table. He wanted this be a no-guilt decision.

Rebecca looked groggy and half asleep, with a crease on one of her cheeks, a bit of dried drool on the corner of her mouth, and her bangs stuck straight in the air. She twisted in her seat and spoke over her arm to Sarah in the next booth. "Didn't I tell you, Sarah? I said, 'This guy is going to be trouble with his dimples and tattoos and those abs.' I said, 'Yum,' and I said, 'He's going to cause nothing but trouble. He'll smile at me and then I'll do anything he wants.'"

Sarah raised her head off Dan's shoulder joined in pretending as if Beckett wasn't there. "You did say exactly that, but if you'll remember I disagreed; I said he wasn't your type. He was neither pasty enough, doughy enough, nor was he a comic book reader. I told you you would be fine."

Rebecca sighed. "We *are* done with the research we needed, everything else is just cake."

Sarah said, "That it is."

Rebecca said, "And he wants to ride into a storm for love. How am I supposed to say no to that — so I can continue to celebrate that my research is over?"

Sarah said, "My head wants to vote 'no' on the 'continuing to celebrate.' And it *is* for love."

"What about you, Dr Mags? Any reason why we shouldn't let Beckett talk me into this romantic folly?"

Dr Mags said, "Well I didn't want to mention it before, but this has been a pretty boring trip, you know, except for the whales, and the turtles, and the injuries, and the nomads. When I think about it most of the exciting things that have happened have been because of Beckett. So, why not?"

"Jeffrey?"

Jeffrey bobbed his head, "Not a big fan of storms, but I'll do what everyone else wants."

"Okay, Dan?"

"One of my basic life principles is to never ask an Army guy what direction my ship should be pointing." He grinned and tightened his arm around Sarah's shoulder. "That being said, I'm a sucker for a romantic story, aren't I baby?"

Sarah kissed his jawline. "You cried like a baby at our wedding."

"True that. I'm in."

Rebecca dramatically sighed and turned to Beckett. "You want me to agree to riding into the storm so you can save this love of your life?"

Beckett smiled. "If you want I can bring up my Calvin and Hobbes comic book, prove that I'm a comic book nerd to sweeten the deal." He batted his eyes and made his dimple really dimple.

Rebecca laughed, begrudgingly. "Fine. But now that we're in close proximity, I see you really aren't my type at all. Sarah was right, despite the epic tattoos — I've always dreamed of a guy with an eagle on his back — you aren't doughy enough. I definitely shouldn't be with someone cuter than me. So, fine. We'll go rescue your girlfriend. Definitely."

"Thank you." Beckett stood. "Thank you so much everyone, I don't deserve this much, but Luna does, thank you." He raced up the steps to tell captain Aria to pretty please sail their ship into the Sierra Squalls.

Chapter 10

The rain slowed to a steady downpour. Relentless but not as threatening. A lot less loud. Luna stuck her head out of her tent and looked around. The whole place looked flattened, like a giant had stepped on her camp, crushed everything, and left pooled water, six inches deep in most places, including a fresh pond pressing against the tent.

Her tent was damming a newly formed lake. Great.

She climbed out and sloshed a few feet away to pee, then poop. Rain poured down her face. There weren't any dry spots because most of the tree limbs were down. Crash! — another branch fell causing Luna to scramble her pants back up and dive for the tent. She huddled around her knees.

Night was coming on.

Nothing she could do about any of this until tomorrow.

She hadn't even been out long enough to check her boards.

But then again, did she really want to know?

Chapter 11

The H2OPE followed the tail end of the storm as it swept through the Sierra Islands. A bank of clouds blustered and preened up ahead, looking mighty and terrifying, but Beckett tried not to look. Captain Aria aimed for the coordinates — where Luna might be. Possibly.

Dan explained that squalls in this area would sit on one spot and stir for three days. He called it "plaguing." Which seemed apt. There would be a break of seven days, and three more days of squall again. The whole season.

Luna had picked the wrong week.

Her safety depended on how long it took her to get through this area. But also, no one should ever try to paddle board through the Sierra Islands. Not during squall season. Not without a backup plan.

Beckett was the backup plan, except there wasn't a plan, just finding her again, in a different part of the massive ocean.

But Beckett was grateful the storm was gone. It would have sucked if the ship had been pitching and tossing in a storm that he asked the crew to sail into. But also, the storm was past. Had passed. If something had happened to Luna in the storm, it was probably too late. Probably.

According to the coordinates, Luna was near here, or had been on that last day. Possibly one of these (many) inlets.

The H2OPE anchored offshore in the evening and sent up a few flares.

Dan drove Beckett in the Zodiac to the two closest inlets, but Luna wasn't to be found. Dark came on. They returned to the ship without her and the only thing to do was be patient. Morning. They would search more at first light.

Beckett and Dan sat in one of the booths in the galley and Dan asked, "Are you sure she's worth it? I mean, I get that we have to save her life, but are you sure about the whole other part?"

Beckett said, "I'm sure. I've never been more sure."

"But how do you know — you just met her, right?"

Beckett held a glass of water, feeling the now familiar pitch and roll of the ocean under him. "You know how the world feels tragically wrong, you're following orders and trying to get through to your next duty? I met Luna and she made me forget all of that. I forget to be worried when I'm with her. But also, and this doesn't make a lot of sense, I want to make sure she's okay."

Dan dropped into the booth. "Before Sarah, I was going to reenlist, ten more years because I had nothing, no family, no home. I figured I might as well go East and die in the war. At least I'd die with honor. Because I had nothing else. Until I met Sarah and her work, and now I'm a cook, saving the whales, waking up with her in my arms — now I have something."

"Luna's my something. And I have to find her."

Dan nodded "Okay then, I ought to stop asking questions and help you." And with that Dan went to bed and a few deep breaths later, Beckett followed him to the bunks.

Chapter 12

Dan drove the Zodiac, while Beckett perched in the front, scanning, searching, occasionally calling, "Luna! Luna!"

He thought he'd see her boards, tied up in the water, possibly dragged up a little way, although he wasn't sure. He wondered if Waterfolk would hide their boards while they were on land and wished he knew anything, anything at all. He called "Luna!" As the Zodiac sped buzzing around the rocky outcropping of a small island. Dan slowed down as they putted close, scanning the beach. Beckett cupped his hands around his mouth and yelled, "Luna!" again.

Chapter 13

Luna's eyes jerked open. That was an engine, buzzing, in the distance. Her heart raced. Crap. She was alone. Alone alone. There was a chance that the engine had a friendly person attached to it. A helpful, kind, generous person. But that chance was very very small. Her breath gasped. She glanced around the broken tent at her sopping wet EVERYTHNG. There was a real possibility that Luna, alone, was in a dangerous situation. Best case scenario? She lost her stuff. Worst case? Crap. She definitely didn't want any worse cases.

But it was seriously hard to think this all through because her head, her heart, her mind, were all broken. That was the only explanation for how she felt: broke, near-drowned, sodden, desperate. Maybe she could stand on the edge of the water and wave her arms and beg to be taken on board. Surrender.

God, she wasn't capable of this. She wasn't strong or brave or —

She grabbed the radio (battery dead because of the lack of sun), her wet sack, and the water desalination kit with Beckett's name scrawled on it, unzipped the tent, looked both ways, and lugged it all to the tree line, hurrying, splashing through ankle deep puddles all the way. When she made it to the tree line, she shoved further in through the underbrush and stashed everything under a bushy mass of ferns. She tried to calm her mind and breath to listen — the engine still sounded very far away.

She raced back and yanked up the tent's stakes, her body moving without her brains, heaved a corner of the tent (still pretty full of gear), and dragged it through the muck to the hiding spot under the trees. The tent billowed. She threw her body on top, begging the tent to collapse, but it obstinately continued being a tent. "Damn it, deflate, tent. Deflate." She twisted and folded it, and dragged it farther into the woods, hoping it couldn't be seen. It was bright yellow — it needed to be dark and easy to hide.

The engine was coming closer — she dropped down beside the tent and wrapped her arms around her knees and pressed her kneecaps into her eyes — if it made it to the inlet, it would see her boards for sure — Breathe gasp breathe gasp breathe gasp breathe —

Chapter 14

Beckett's voice was hoarse. "What I need is a bullhorn."

"I don't think she could hear you over the engine anyways. And she can hear the engine. She'll come out."

Would she? That seemed like another bit of Waterfolk information that Beckett lacked. Did Nomadic Waterfolk trust strangers on motorized boats? When Beckett had lived on the Outpost he had found them to be very untrusting. Of him, personally, perhaps especially.

They turned into another inlet. This looked more promising. So far the islands had been banked with cliffs, or other inhabitable outcroppings, but this one had a sloping hill, trees, ferns, even rocks to tie off her boards. But there weren't any boards. They puttered the engine and scanned the hill above.

"I should get out. Check the hill there."

"Sure," Dan spun the Zodiac to the right and deftly up against a rock. "Step careful."

Beckett climbed from the rocking Zodiac to the slanting rock and then scaled it, trying to look casual and knowledgeable. He jumped from the rocks to land. This would be a perfect inlet. He scaled the hill, jumping across small gullies, pushing aside dripping limbs, slipping in mud, to the top and looked down. There were plenty of places to harbor, but no signs of life. After scanning the hill and around at the horizon he jogged, slipping and sliding, back to the Zodiac.

Dan asked, "Next one?"

Chapter 15

Dan drove the Zodiac around yet another small island and into a tree covered inlet — Beckett yelled, "A board, wait — Luna's board. It's right there!" He stood, the Zodiac rocking under his excitement.

Dan said, "Hold on Romeo, don't swim it, that's why we have a boat."

"It's right there!" Beckett scanned up and down the hill. A waterfall rushed down the middle of the slope. The banks of the river were fern-lined. Further along was a wooded area. No sign of Luna.

Her board, Steve, was right here, but… he half-stood and peered around. Luna's trailing board, Boosy, was crashed against some rocks. It did not look good. The pot was overturned. Tree was —

His heart raced. The hill was deserted. Dan pulled to a boulder, and Beckett leaped from the boat as Dan tied it off. Dan called, "I'm coming too."

"Good, I'm going to the top." Beckett bounded up the sloping terrain, jumping back and forth across the downward rushing gully, stumbling and splashing.

Dan scrambled up the hill toward the woods. He was ankle deep in mud so he jogged, splashing through a marshy muck-filled field. He reached the tree line as Beckett yelled, "Nothing, nobody — you see anything?"

Dan peered into the heavily shadowed woods. He crept through the darkness, searching. Something looked weird — a billowing shape glowed a bit farther in. He moved closer to inspect it and found a sopping, overturned, twisted, broken, tent.

"A tent!" Dan spun and caught sight of a lump of a person huddled around her knees, it took two steps to get to her. Luna, her hands pressed to her ears.

He reached out and touched her shoulder and she started screaming.

Chapter 16

Luna pushed away, screaming and holding her ears, her eyes clamped shut. Dan said, "Hey, I'm with—" Luna pulled farther away, her screams loud and terrible and terrified.

Dan clutched her shoulder, afraid she might fight or run away.

He yelled, "Beckett!" Footsteps thundered down the hill and splashed through the ferns.

Beckett dropped to his knees and grabbed her by the shoulders. Her screams grew louder and more frantic. "It's me. It's me Beckett."

He tried to pull her toward his chest, but she sobbed and shoved and struggled, and frantically tried to get away. "Stop! I've got to go I have to paddle, I have to paddle — stop, you're hurting me!" She swung wildly and scratched Beckett across the face.

"Luna! It's me!" His breath was coming fast and shallow. He was close to panicking.

Dan said, "Jeez, do you see how much she's shivering?"

"Yeah, I see." Her arm swung out and Beckett dove under it, struggling to keep her close.

"Look man, try to hold her. Try and get her calm."

"I'm trying, I'm freaking —"

Dan moved into Beckett's focus. "Look at me, in the eyes—don't freak, you can do this. I'm going for the blanket thingy and the kit." Dan raced to the boat.

Beckett said, "Shhhhh, shhhh, Luna, shhhh."

Her eyes were wild. "I have to go, I promised. I have to—" Her eyes fell on her broken twisted tent. She blinked. "I have to—" She looked over her shoulder in the direction of the water. "I have to get my boards. I have to — I need to—"

She collapsed and cowered, low and frightened, covered in mud from head to toe, twigs in her hair. Beckett reached out for her shoulder. "Luna, I—"

She screamed.

"Luna!"

"Stop touching me, I need to go! To Heighton Port, Beckett is meet—" She faltered and looked around confused.

Dan rushed into the clearing and dropped to his knees. He ripped a vacuum sealed bag with his teeth and a blanket erupted with a puff. Beckett scrambled forward, grasped Luna by the shoulders, and pulled her to his chest, "Shhhh, shhhh. Don't be scared."

Dan threw the blanket over Luna and wordlessly tucked it tightly around her body.

She stared around, blank eyed and trembling. "I don't — I have to get to Beckett—" Suddenly, she pulled her head up. "Why are you here?"

"I came to get you, because—"

She shoved away hard on his chest, her eyes wild and confused again. "I told you I got this, I said I was coming, I promised, I said I got this—" She scrambled against a tree trunk, like she wanted to escape.

"I came because I was worried about the—"

"I — I — I don't need to be rescued."

Dan said, "Hey Luna, it's cool, we didn't come to rescue you, we just happened to be in the neighborhood. Checking to see if you wanted a ride."

Luna said, "I have to pack up. I have to paddle to meet Beckett. I have to—"

Beckett crawled over and pulled her close. He rubbed the back of her head and down her shoulders. "Shhhh. Shhhh. It's going to be okay." He draped the blanket and tucked it around her body.

She said, "It's not — it won't."

Dan pulled a package out of the medical kit and unwrapped a syringe.

Luna clutched Beckett's shirt, sobbing into his chest. "I tied the knot. I did. I tied it and — it was a good knot. I promised. I know it was — I—"

Dan pushed up the bottom of the blanket exposing Luna's leg and counted, wordlessly, "One two three." Beckett wrapped his arms around Luna's arms. "Shhhhh. Shhhh."

Dan jabbed the needle in Luna's thigh.

Luna looked shocked then burrowed deeper into Beckett's arms, whimpering.

Beckett repeated softly, "Shhhhh. Shhhhh." Until finally Luna's eyes rolled back in her head. She grew heavy, and her head lolled forward, asleep.

Dan said, "Phew." He gestured to the syringe. "I asked Dr Mags why sedatives were in the kit. If it was for me when I get belligerent and horny with Sarah, and she said I would need it if I needed it. I guess this is what she meant, huh?"

Beckett nodded and carefully shifted Luna to the ferns at his side. He wrapped the blanket tightly around her and sat for a second staring at her face. He shook his head slowly. "Man, this sucks."

"I thought you were going to lose it."

Beckett clutched his chest. "I thought so too, it was hard to breathe." He felt his cheek.

"You've got a big scratch. It'll mar your good looks for a while, keep you humble."

Beckett let out another big gust of air.

Dan asked, "You know what she meant about that knot?"

"Nope."

Dan clapped him on the shoulder. "Well, you've got a lot to learn, huh?"

"We need to pack up all this stuff and get her to the ship."

Chapter 17

Luna's tent was broken and torn, her paddleboard had only sustained some dings, but her trailer board, Boosy, was cracked almost in two. Tree needed to be repotted or it wouldn't survive. Luna's desalinization kit was a muddy wreck. Her food was soggy. Most of it they piled on the deck of the H2OPE so that Luna and Beckett could make sense of it all once she woke up.

Luna was carried into a room off the lab and deposited onto a cot. Dr Mags and Sarah bathed her. Dr Mags said, "We have to let her sleep it off. When she wakes up, we'll see what we shall see."

Beckett asked, "What time will she wake up?"

"Probably morning. But I'll stay here with her for a few hours and—"

"I'll stay here tonight." Beckett glanced around the cramped storage room. He'd be on the floor.

Beckett returned to the upper deck where the crew were appraising the pile of stuff that Luna used to paddle the ocean. It was small. Pitiful in its broken state. As was Luna, pitiful, broken. Beckett shook at the memory of her wild eyes. He ran his hands around and around on top of his head.

Sarah gave him a pitying smile.

Rebecca asked Dan, "Isn't it time for dinner?"

Dan said, "I'll whip up something in a moment."

Rebecca, Jeffrey, and Sarah headed to the lab to get some more work done.

Dan and Beckett stood staring at Luna's stuff. Dan said, "How you holding together, that was pretty brutal back there."

"Not good."

"The good news is your instincts were correct. You had to come. She was not going to live through this. Her board is wrecked. She couldn't figure that all out in her state."

"Yep, I rescued her fair and square, so why do I feel like shit?"

Dan nodded. "I know. Is she pretty forgiving?"

Beckett shrugged. "We'll see when she wakes up."

Dan clapped his hand on Beckett's shoulder. "She's incredibly brave to head out on the ocean with only this, alone. So you have to trust that she'll make it out of wherever she just was. You did the right thing."

"It's the alone part, that's what did it."

"She's not alone anymore, she has us. And speaking of us, come help me in the kitchen, I have to feed everyone."

Chapter 18

Beckett whispered, "Is she still sleeping?"

Dr Mags nodded, stood, and stretched. "Did Dan whip up one of his gourmet dinners?"

"Beans and weenies. He kept a plate warm for you."

"Can't wait to get back to shore for some steak. How about you?"

"Pizza."

Dr Mags said, "Use the intercom if she wakes up. Needs anything."

"Absolutely." Dr Mags switched off the overhead light, leaving the room bathed in the glow of moonlight, and left. Beckett dropped to a cramped space beside the cot.

Luna was flat on her back. Her mouth hung open, and damp hair was pasted to her forehead. She looked pale. Her eyes had dark rings around them. Beckett found her hand under the blanket and clutched it in both of his. He whispered, "Hey Luna, it's me Beckett."

He listened to her soft breath — in and out and in and out.

"You scared the hell out of me back there. Seriously." He dropped his forehead to the back of her hand. "I need you to come back. Okay? Be Luna, be ocean goddess. The kind of person who will paddle across the ocean, but you don't have to anymore. Okay? Not unless you want to. But you don't have to."

She stirred for a second. He watched her face, but she resumed her soft breathing. "And if you want to tell me about the knot, you can. It's okay. You can tell me anything."

A few hours later Luna shifted and moaned startling Beckett awake. She was still sleeping, but moaned again. He stretched out his sore back. He had been sleeping sitting up, on a towel folded on the metal floor. His back was killing him, making him miss his bunk, a mattress that until tonight had been the most uncomfortable mattress he had ever slept on. "Luna?"

No answer. He said, "Luna I'm here. It's me, Beckett."

Her fingers tightened around his hand so he kissed her knuckles and tried to go back to sleep.

More hours passed and Luna had grown restless. Beckett watched her shift and move. She seemed like she was waking, but unable to open her eyes, as if she was stuck in a half sleep. He imagined what it would be like to wake up here now after the day (Week? Month? Year?) she had lived through. In the dark, on a boat, surrounded by strangers. Beckett leering at her. Did she hate him now?

Luna rolled to her side, still sleeping, but facing him. That seemed hopeful, more comfortable, more like sleep, instead of the medicated forced-pass-out of before. He put his head back down on his arms on the edge of her cot and tried to sleep some more.

———————————

"Beckett?"

He jerked awake. "Luna? You're awake."

"Beckett?"

Her eyes were open, but unfocused — she sounded disoriented.

He said, "Yes, I'm right here."

"Beckett?" Her face screwed up, tears flowed down her cheek onto her fingertips. "I'm so sorry, I was going to come."

"I know you were." She stilled, as if she hadn't expected him to speak.

He rose up on his knees and wrapped his hands around her hands. "You were coming and you were halfway there but there was a storm. And none of it was your fault, but now you're on my ship. With me. Safe."

He yawned, a giant convulsive yawn.

She said, "I'm so sorry. I'm so sorry."

"About what?"

She said, "The knot. I didn't—" Her voice sounded desperately sad. "I should have been better. I should have—" she covered her face with her hands and her shoulder shook with sobs.

"But now you're safe. And you need to sleep now, and when you wake up, you'll feel better." Beckett hoped it was true. Her confusion and tears frightened him to his core.

"Can you hold me?"

He nodded, pushed her a bit to the side and slid onto the cot. He slipped his arm under her body and pulled her head to his chest. Her fingers twisted in his shirt, and she cried there for a long long time.

Chapter 19

Beckett woke, there was a heavyweight on his chest, a strange light, and a disorienting vibe. Where was he? Oh, right, he was with — he lifted his head and Luna was lying on his chest, looking up.

"Hi."

"Hi."

He lifted her arm to shift her weight. His left side had gone numb.

She said, "Beckett."

He smiled. "Yep. It's me."

She nodded her chin rubbing on his chest. "I thought so, but I wasn't sure if you were a dream."

He propped his head up with an arm. "One hundred percent."

"Good." She put her head on his chest and nestled in for a moment. Her fingers traced lazy circles on his t-shirt. Then her head came up and she asked, "Can you tell me what happened?"

"Just that after you disappeared from the radio, I went to find you, and here you are."

She blinked a couple of times. "The longer version, please."

"Dan and I were in the Zodiac, searching inlets until we saw your boards, we found your tent, then you, and we transported you to the ship. You've been sleeping since yesterday."

She reached up and touched his cheek. "This scratch on your cheek? I think I need the very, possibly excruciating, longer version."

He stared at the ceiling, choosing his words. "You were really scared, screaming, you struggled to get away. I thought you were going to—" He looked down at her face. "Are you sure you want to hear it?"

She nodded.

"I tried to calm you down, to hold you still so you could hear me, but you were screaming and talking about me — *to* me."

"I did this?"

Beckett touched his cheek. "This is nothing Luna, don't worry about it." He said, "We administered a sedative to calm you down, so we could get you to the boat. There was no other way."

She squinted her eyes. "You darted me? That's why my thigh is sore?"

Beckett nodded solemnly. "I'm sorry. I couldn't think of what else…"

Luna smiled a slow sad smile. "Well, one thing, it makes our love story really weird. So that's cool."

Beckett smiled with relief, flashing her a dimple. "You aren't pissed? I thought you would be pissed."

"No. But let's not allow it to become a precedent."

"Deal."

"The whole story please."

"You collapsed, and Dan and I packed up your things. Or rather, not packed but bundled and carried them. Then I carried you. You were bathed." Luna held up a hand, investigating the mud caked around her nails and her wrist. "Not necessarily well, and you were checked by

Dr Mags, and now you've been sleeping for hours and hours."

"While you waited to see if I would wake up like a screaming banshee again?"

"The possibility crossed my mind."

Luna nodded slowly and stared into his eyes. "I'm sorry I scared you."

Luna put her head back down and resumed the spinning fingers on his shirt. "And Steve? Boosy? Tree? Did they make it?"

Beckett gulped. "Steve seems fine. But you'll — Boosy is—"

"Don't tell me, I'll see it. It's fine."

She sniffled and lay quietly for a few minutes.

Quietly she said, "I think I'm more trouble than I'm worth."

Beckett's head jerked up. "What?"

"I'm too much trouble for you that you—"

"Luna." He stroked a finger down her cheek. "Look at me."

She hid her face in his side. "I don't want to. You're going to say nice things because you have to, but I'm not worth it. You don't know me. I'm just nobody."

"Oh god, Luna, you're saying this to me? You aren't nobody, you're everything — look at me, please."

She raised her head, tears rolling down her cheeks.

"You have caused me a tremendous amount of trouble, that much is true. But I've caused you trouble too. You would have been safe if you'd stayed with Sky, but I asked you to leave. The two of us, so far, one big wreck. For each other."

"Kind of like the little boy and the tiger when they crash the wagon?"

Beckett nodded and smiled. "Exactly like that, like Calvin and Hobbes. We crashed our wagon into a tree and we're sitting up and looking around and agreeing that mistakes were made, but guess what we're going to do?"

"Roll the wagon back up the hill?"

"My house is waiting for us. And I'm Calvin by the way. Ask Calvin how he would feel living without the tiger."

"Thank you." She shifted up Beckett's body, steadied his cheeks and kissed him sweetly. Her cheeks were wet with tears and her lips were salty and she smelled like earth and fear and he wanted to hold her forever, but also, he needed to get up and use the bathroom. So he said, "Dr Mags wants to give you a look. I'll send her in."

Chapter 20

Luna arrived in the galley before Beckett. She was showered clean, dewy damp, and wrapped in Beckett's great great-great-great grandmother's quilt.

Sarah was sitting in one of the booths, stacks of paper in front of her. She looked up. "Oh, good morning, come have a seat. Dan!"

Dan appeared around the corner. "Hi, um, Luna, I'm Dan, we met when I gave you the radio?"

Luna smiled. "Also when you helped Beckett dart me with a sedative."

He grimaced, "Oh, um yeah."

Sarah raised her brows. "I told him you were going to give him hell about that. I'm Sarah." She held out a hand.

"I would, they definitely deserve it, but also they saved my life, so it's hard to give them the grief they deserve. Instead Beckett and I have agreed that going forward — no tranquilizer darts."

Dan chuckled, "Hear that, baby? Beckett's girl forgave him for the dart. I told you. What do — um, Nomads, like to drink for breakfast?"

Luna said, "We prefer to be called Waterfolk, and I'll have dolphin milk if you have it." She plopped down in the empty booth. "But if you're out of dolphin milk then coffee. Three scoops of sugar please. And do you have chocolate?"

Dan grinned. "Now see, I did not know you had a sense of humor. We'll have fun me and you." He disappeared into the kitchen.

Sarah said, "That's awesome Luna, you made him falter. That's pretty rare."

Rebecca clattered down the steps.

Sarah said, "Happy Birthday Rebecca!"

"Why thank you kindly. Are we going to celebrate later? Dinner?"

Sarah nodded.

Dan stuck his head around the corner. "Party! Party! Party!"

Rebecca said, "Hi Luna, you're up? I'm Rebecca." She held out her hand and they shook.

Luna said, "Happy birthday."

"Thanks, you'll have to come to my party of course. It's literally the only thing happening."

Sarah said, "Our new friend Luna here, caused Dan to become speechless earlier."

"Seriously?" Rebecca smiled widely. "I'm going to sit and enjoy the show, but also, Luna, I want to ask you a million questions—"

Dan returned with her coffee and a plate piled with cheesy eggs and 6 pieces of toast. "Rebecca how about you let her eat first?"

Luna dug into the food, shoving heaping spoonfuls of eggs into her mouth.

Dan said, "Plus, I have questions first, starting with, how many miles a day can you paddle?"

Luna chewed a bit and swallowed it down. "Spring, with a blustery side-pushing wind? Or Fall, with a current pushing from behind?"

Dan grinned. "I don't know, average."

"Forty miles."

"Forty miles? Forty, that's your average?"

"Depends on the current, the wind, my mood, and my family—" She faltered for a second. "Everyone around me, how fast they're going. But yes, forty miles. Easy."

"Easy?" Dan leaned back. "You're a freaking ocean god. Sarah, do you hear this? We have a superhero on the ship. Can you take me out Luna, show me how?"

Beckett came down the steps, beaming. That was Luna. Here, eating breakfast. Wrapped in his quilt. He said, "Dr Mags checked my hands, said they were better. The bandage is smaller." He held them up and wiggled his fingers as he slid into the booth. He wrapped an arm through hers. She nestled her head onto his shoulder.

He asked, "You good?"

"Well let's see, I feel better. I'm clean, dry and alive. You. And there's a birthday party tonight, plus my new friend called me an 'Ocean God,' so, yes. But especially you."

He kissed the top of her damp forehead.

Chapter 21

After breakfast Luna went up to the main deck and solemnly looked at her pile of LITERALLY EVERYTHING SHE OWNED.

Beckett lifted some sodden fabric off the pile. "This is your stuff, with some twigs and mud."

"It looks so sad."

"That's exactly how I would describe it."

"Boosy is not supposed to have a crack through his middle."

"That wasn't how I remembered him."

Tree was on the ground. Luna gingerly lifted the trunk and felt around the root ball. "Maybe with some new dirt?"

"Possibly. We can get some when we stop. We're going to the southern end of the islands, then straight home to Heighton Port."

Luna scrunched up her face. "That's earlier by a few days."

"True. It's easier to go back to Port than to stay out."

"So because of me?"

"Probably more like because of me. I have some amends to make for coming aboard in the first place."

"I'll help you make them."

Luna lifted the edge of her tent and scooped out a pile of soggy moldy smelling fabric. "Oh, my clothes." She dug through the pile until she found the edge of a dark green shirt. She clutched it to her chest. "Good, your shirt is still here. I thought—"

"I have more."

"Not this one. This one is mine fair and square. I scavenged it from the Outpost. Plus. . ." She tugged at a knot in the middle and spilled something into her palm. "It has your grandfather's watch." She held it toward him.

"You can keep it."

"Nope. It was to remind me of you. Now I have you, so it's yours again. But I keep the shirt."

Beckett secured the watch on his wrist and grinned. "See, now I'm super glad I came to get you."

Captain Aria appeared and Beckett introduced her to Luna. She asked, "Are you feeling better? You were completely out when you arrived."

Luna said, "I have a headache, and I was famished, but I've eaten now. Thank you for that, and for everything, really. I'm so grateful to be here and sorry about all the trouble I caused."

Captain Aria nodded. "You're welcome. But as a Captain on the high seas I have a duty to rescue other vessels that I come across. I had to go out of my way to come across you, but that is simply a matter of semantics. And as long as my researchers were okay with the diversion, and they were, it was nothing but directing my vessel in a new direction."

"I hope that my being here hasn't gotten Beckett in trouble. He…"

Captain Aria smirked and spoke to Luna ignoring Beckett. "Let's just say that since Beckett came on board he has made it exciting around here. Yet, somehow, he has ingratiated himself with everyone on board. It could be his incompetence as a seaman made him comedic relief, or his helplessness because of his injuries gave us a common cause, or his desperation to find you, but I suspect it's his dimples. We hope to get him to shore before his smile causes real damage to this ship and crew."

Luna smiled. "He ingratiated himself to me too."

"I suppose he has what with all that heroism and all. And speaking of heroes. I've been out here three times this morning looking at this pile, marveling really. You travel out on the ocean with this little amount gear. I have been thinking about what I believe is essential to ocean travel and how none of that is in this pile. You really don't use any communication or location equipment?"

"No, we have ways of navigating and traveling without it."

"What about in emergencies, like if you find yourself alone?"

Luna gulped and looked down at the deck. "I guess generally we think it's too heavy for just in case. Unnecessary."

Captain Aria asked, "What about now, do you still think that?"

"I know how to navigate by the stars, but it's communicating over the distances, asking for help. That's what's so difficult."

"I imagine so."

Chapter 22

Beckett stood at the upper railing watching Luna and Dan and Jeffrey on the level below, suiting up to get into the water. Or rather Dan and Jeffrey were suiting up, Luna had on simple yoga pants and top. Her paddle board, Steve, and the Zodiac had been lowered down in the water. Dan climbed down the ladder after Jeffrey.

Luna casually said, "You're going down the ladder, huh? Pretty Stiffneck of you."

Dan looked up. "What, but — how are you going to get in?"

Luna looked up at Beckett with a question in her eyes.

He called down, "Don't worry about me, I won't look." He turned away from the railing as Sarah walked up and asked, "Are they in the water already?"

There was a big splash.

Luna came up and yelled, "Whoooo! Beckett I'm good!"

Beckett turned back to the water and waved.

Dan said, "If I had known you were going to jump, I would have jumped too."

Luna effortlessly lifted herself to the paddleboard and circled the Zodiac, giving Dan a lesson on holding the paddle and standing. Then she crawled effortlessly into the Zodiac while Dan moved to the paddleboard and sent it rocking. "Why's it so small?" He got to his knees and sat there for a moment. "You made this look easy."

Luna laughed, "It is. It's totally easy. Just stand up."

Dan got on his hands and knees trying to get a foot under him with the board shifting and rocking until he slid into the water.

Sarah laughed and spoke to Beckett. "This is so fun to watch. It's going to drive him crazy that she's better at this than him."

Beckett said, "He'll never get better than her, so he'll need to get used to it."

"Never, but he'll have fun trying."

Dan climbed back on with the paddleboard rocking up and down. He asked Luna, "Okay, how?"

Luna laughed and shook her head. "Put one foot under you and then the other."

Dan jokingly glowered at her. "Very funny. The ground is moving." He rose struggling and splashing until he had his feet under him, but was bent in half at the waist.

Luna laughed. "Now you have to stand up straight, but loose."

"I'm not standing?" His top half was practically parallel with the board.

Luna cocked her head to the side. "Maybe? Can you see the horizon?"

"No! I can only see the board!"

Luna giggled. "Okay that's probably fine, let's call that standing. Now put your paddle in the water and push it back."

Dan lowered the paddle to the water, lost his balance, spun his arms, dropped the paddle, it started floating away, and overturned the board. He hit the water with a giant, arms spiraling splash.

He came up with a whoosh and pulled his top half up on the board with a grin. "Was I doing it?"

Luna deftly fished the paddle out of the water. "Dan, I say this with kindness and gratitude, but it must be said — if you're under the water, you're not doing it right."

He hoisted himself back to the board with a laugh.

He and Luna practiced for an hour. Dan finally got the hang of it and Jeffrey and Luna followed him in the Zodiac and returned him to the ship a while later. Dan climbed the ladder and called down over his shoulder to Luna still sitting in the Zodiac. "That is so tiring. How far did I go?"

Luna called up. "Um, about a half mile?"

He laughed and called up to Sarah, "Did you see me, baby?"

She laughed, "I did, you looked like an ocean god battling your arch nemesis, gravity."

Dan climbed to the deck and flung the water from his hair. "I see how you guys are. Beckett do you hear how the love of my life is talking to me?"

"I do, you should have awed her into silence by showing your ass."

"My luck is I'd get court-martialed. I'm not cute enough to get away with any of that."

Dan towel-dried his hair as he left for the galley. "I have a birthday cake to make. Better get busy."

Beckett watched Luna, remembering the first day when she paddled into his life, much like this, cheeky smile, paddling in lazy circles. She watched the horizon while Beckett watched her. Finally, she turned her board to the ship, shielded her eyes from the sun, and called up, "Beckett can you call Rebecca out?"

Beckett and Sarah both yelled, "Rebecca!"

Rebecca appeared a moment later, wiping her hands on a towel. "Yes?"

Beckett gestured down at Luna, who called up, "Rebecca can you put on your bathing suit and come down? I have something to show you."

"Me? My bathing suit?"

Luna grinned. "Come on, it will be worth it. And go quick, bring your camera."

Rebecca raced into the lab and came back a few minutes later in yoga pants and a bathing suit top. As she passed Beckett she asked, "Do you know what it is?"

Sarah said, "I think she's taking you out paddleboarding."

"Oh." She climbed down the ladder to the lower deck and asked, "Should Jeffrey or Dan come, bring the Zodiac?"

Luna said, "Nope, the engines would scare what I'm showing you."

"Really, what? Is it something cool, something big — tell me Luna."

"It's a birthday surprise and you're going to miss it if you don't jump."

Rebecca took Luna seriously and instead of going down the ladder did an awkward jump out with an arm-flapping descent. She swam two short strokes to Luna who lifted her under her arms to the board and somehow kept them both balanced. Rebecca kneeled at the front and Luna paddled to the horizon fast, calling over her shoulder, "We'll be back in a few minutes! Don't leave!"

———

They were gone for over an hour. When they returned, Rebecca was exuberant. She began talking way before she got to the boat and continued nonstop. "Whales everyone, whales, Luna took me to see whales. And how do you think she saw them? She was paddling and noticed the water current. Then she saw a school of fish. She followed it with her eyes and in the distance she noticed a splash and she just knew. That's all it took. She paddled me out there right in the middle of a pod." Luna held the ladder while Rebecca climbed from the paddleboard. "Did you see how far away we were? Could you see the flukes?"

Sarah said, "I didn't see anything. How many were there?"

"I think seven. One of them came so close I could have touched it. Gray whales." She stood beside them on the deck. "It was the most amazing thing I ever saw." She called down, "Luna do you need help?"

Luna laughed as she pushed the paddleboard into the sling to be lifted to the ship. "Nope, carry on." She climbed the ladder and joined Beckett. "I want to take you to see them, but I'm very tired, do you mind?"

Beckett said, "I understand, we have always."

Rebecca said, "That was the most amazing birthday present I've ever had, thank you so much Luna. It meant the world to me. That was, wow."

"I'm happy to do it. You really haven't seen that many? It must be the engines."

"Really? Maybe we need paddleboards for the next trip. Come on Sarah, I want to go tell Jeffrey about it." They wandered off.

Luna's mouth gaped open in a big loud yawn.

Beckett laughed. "How about I show you to my bunk so you can nap? I have about ten more chores to finish before I help everyone with the birthday party prep."

Chapter 23

Sarah and Jeffrey had decorated the upper deck beautifully with small twinkle lights and a birthday sign. Everyone had taken showers and gotten as pretty as they could get on board a ship.

At the agreed upon time they all clambered down the steps to the galley where Dan served heaping plates of orange pork with rice. Then they carried their plates to the deck to eat and drink in the moonlight with the open starry sky and the twinkly lights all around. They balanced plates on their laps and laughed and talked and Dr Mags turned on some of Rebecca's music, a country musician named Pun Winston, causing Rebecca to clap happily.

Sarah rolled her eyes. "Again?"

Rebecca said, "My favorite — my birthday."

After they were finished eating, Dan and Jeffrey took the piles of plates back to the kitchen and returned a few minutes later carrying a platter covered in a pile of small cakes with a candle burning in the middle. As soon as Dan's foot hit the deck, he began singing a birthday song and everyone joined in, except Luna who watched, smiling, not knowing the words. Jeffrey begged everyone to use their hands to eat the cake because he, "Did not want to do this many dishes," but Dan refused to, "Eat like barbarians," and passed out more plates and forks, assuring everyone that, "Jeffrey will clean up everything. Don't worry about it."

After the cake, Dr Mags turned the music up louder, some fancy mixed shots were passed to everyone who wanted to drink, and the laughing grew louder. Beckett requested a song by Blaise Portnoy and held out his hand to Luna who took it with a grin, and they did their sexy dance from the Outpost but with a lot of giggling, because Jeffrey was dancing a jig with Rebecca beside them, Dan was dancing with Captain Aria, Sarah was dancing with Lenny, and Dr Mags was dancing around alone through them all. In between songs, everyone except Beckett and Luna drank another shot, traded dance partners, and danced again and again and again.

Finally exhausted, Luna collapsed in a deck chair and Beckett dropped into the one beside her. Dan dragged one across the deck, and he and Sarah dropped into it wrapping around each other. Captain Aria and Lenny took their leave to go to their quarters. Jeffrey grabbed a chair and Dr Mags returned to the radio and her DJ post. Dan said, "Rebecca! Birthday girl! Say a few words!"

Rebecca stood wobbling a bit. "My friendth, old and new." She hiccuped. "I think I might be a bit tipshy." She giggled. "But I want to say I love you and thank you for my birthday. It was awesome." She looked at her glass and seemed to lose her train of thought, then she said, "This world sucks. Most days. I'm the last one left in my family."

Dr Mags and Dan said, "Hear hear."

Rebecca tossed her pony tail. "I just — I lost them all in the epidemic. And I don't understand why I survived. It doesn't seem fair. Like I shouldn't be here."

Beckett looked over at the side of Luna's face. She was watching Rebecca her eyes wide.

"But then I have days like today, where it seems like there's a reason why I'm still here. Because those whales." She hiccuped and raised her glass toward Luna. "Thank you Luna. That was really good."

A tear streamed down Luna's face.

Rebecca said, "I'm shorry, I brought the mood down."

Sarah said, "That's okay sweetie, we're most of us orphans, we're all of us the last of our line. But we're family now, and we adore you. Happy Birthday."

Everyone raised their glasses and cheered Rebecca as tears spilled from Luna's eyes.

Then Jeffrey said, "I have news — speaking of, you know, orphans and all. I—"

Dan said, "Out with it man, don't leave us hanging here."

Rebecca giggled.

Jeffrey said, "When I get back, I'm enlisted—"

Dan said, "What?"

Sarah said, "Oh no, Jeffrey, no."

Rebecca said, "But you're in school, right? You don't have to go if you're in school, what about your family's land?"

Jeffrey said, "I was graduating from school this year, and I have this cousin, she's got nothing, no land, no family. She's really sweet, and they want to send her to the East. So I decided to go instead. I've had a pretty good time of it. I think it's her turn to enjoy some—"

Rebecca threw herself on his chest sobbing. "Jeffrey, that's the nicest thing I've ever heard, but the East?"

Dan said, "Why the East? Can't you get a cushy assignment like Army here, sandbags?"

Jeffrey said, "I don't have any land or connections to bargain with." He shrugged and looked down at the full shot glass Dr Mags had given him. "It is what it is."

Sarah said, "Jeffrey, you always have a place on our research team, when you come home from the East—"

Rebecca sniffled into Jeffrey's shirt, "Absolutely."

Dan said, "I want to joke something about needing someone to do the dishes, but man, this is tough news. You'll be greatly missed." Everyone raised their shot glasses. "Hear, hear."

Rebecca sat up and sniffled. "Well, since the trip is ending and our crew is splitting up and it's my birthday, and I'm super drunk, I say we must dance again."

Dr Mags turned the volume back up and Jeffrey, Rebecca, Dan, Dr Mags, and Sarah all danced in one big circle with their arms around each other rocking back and forth.

Beckett whispered, "You okay?"

Luna nodded, "I didn't realize how many people are orphaned. How sad they were. I guess I never thought about it."

Beckett nodded solemnly. "I'm an orphan."

Luna looked at him in surprise. "You are? Oh." She looked down at her fingers. "I never asked. I'm sorry."

"That's okay, on land, most people you meet are. The Deep Flu, the one about eighteen years ago, took millions of people. So I guess I'm used to everyone being an orphan. It is what it is."

Luna's looked toward the group, singing a loud drunken song. Her eyes misted as she watched. "Oh."

Beckett asked, "Luna, are you an orphan?"

She closed her eyes and nodded.

Beckett watched the side of her face. "I'm sorry that you are."

Luna bit down on her lips, holding a cry inside. "I guess in the scheme of things it's not that big a deal."

"It is a big deal. It's a very big deal. Thank you for telling me."

The singing group finished their song. Dan slurred, "I gotsta head to bunks, coming baby?"

Sarah laughed, "Someone has to help you so you don't get lost." She threw her arms around Dan and they stumbled giggling to the bunk room.

Rebecca said, "G'night everyone." She hiccuped again. "Dang blast it, that's the third time tonight."

Luna said, "My friend Xylo used to say you have to get hiccups three times before you're done."

Rebecca held up three fingers, lost focus, and slurred, "Magic number — going to bed." She followed Dan and Sarah down to the bunks.

Jeffrey ducked his head. "I have to get to those dishes. It'll probably only take me about two hours. Mind if I take the music down to keep me company?"

Beckett said, "Go for it." Jeffrey grabbed the music and left for the galley.

Luna and Beckett drew their attention up to the starry sky. Luna said, "These people are really great."

"I agree. without them I would have never found you — twice."

Luna reached for his hand, raised it to her lips, and kissed him on the knuckle.

Beckett rolled on his side in his deck chair facing her. "I need to say something, and um, can you hear me out?"

Luna said, "That seems serious."

"It is. I love you. It might not be logical because we just met, but I do. I know our future isn't going to be easy, but whose is these days? But I'm willing to do the work. Maybe that's the logical side of it, we have much to learn about each other, but I'm here, I'm not going any-where."

Luna watched him silently, her dark eyes reflecting the starry sky.

"My offer, that we live in my mountain house, that is always there. But I don't want you to come unless you want to. You don't owe me anything. If you said to me, Beckett, I can't — we would figure that out. And if you can't — with me, that's okay. I will get you back to Sky. You don't need to do this out of gratitude or indebted-ness or anything."

Luna let go of his hand and turned to her side facing him and smiled, curling her hands up under her face. "How would you get me back to Sky?"

Beckett said, "I don't know, um—"

"I'm just asking what the plan would be."

"I guess I would rent a boat."

"You would sea captain a ship to take me back to Sky simply because I said, 'I can't?'"

Beckett nodded solemnly.

Luna shook her head and smiled at him sweetly. "Well, there, my love, it is, the best part about you — you jump, a quality that I happen to adore. If some hot, tat-tooed, dimpled, sweet-talking Stiffneck is going to put out his hand and say, 'jump with me,' I have no response but, 'absolutely.'" She grinned, "But you probably won't hear it because of my splash."

He said, "You understand that I don't jump *literally*, right?"

"Oh, I've seen you jump, *literally*."

"I thought we established that was a belly flop."

"It's the splash that is important, not the style. And you splashed epically."

"It's a lot easier to jump when I don't think about it first."

"Exactly. Stop thinking, my Beckett, don't try to logic all over this. We're going to live in your mountain house. Because you asked. Because you said we. Because it means something all this finding. Plus I love you, how could I not. That's why."

Beckett said, "God, I want you." He crawled from his deck chair across to Luna's, bit by bit, nudging her onto her back, spreading her legs, laying down on her, kissing her —

The door to the steps opened and Sarah stepped out, "Beckett! Luna! Oops!" She covered her eyes and tipsily approached them feeling with her other hand. "So sorry to interrupt. Dan made me come tell you that you should use the Zodiac if you um, want to sleep somewhere, um for privashy, 'kay?"

Luna giggled in Beckett's ear.

Sarah said, "Take it from us, the deck chairs suck, we've tried 'em all."

Beckett asked, "The Zodiac's not wet?"

Sarah said, "Dan is relentleshly hopeful, so he towels it down every day — in case."

Beckett laughed. "I thought that was one of his chores."

Sarah turned away, "I gotta go pass out, have fun kids." She stumbled away.

Beckett looked down into Luna's eyes, "Want to get more comfortable?"

Luna said, "Splash."

Chapter 24

Beckett led Luna by the hand to the Zodiac. It was situated on a lower deck near the front of the ship, and was dark, mostly, one bulb near the ground glowed for safety, but it was directional. Beckett shoved it with his foot to point in the other direction. Luna slithered over the big inflatable side and dropped to the bottom of the boat. "Cushy!"

Beckett climbed over and climbed on top of her, causing her to float up and down as he moved and shifted. They crashed into each other so he scooped his arms around her back and held her close until their rhythm matched. They stilled and the air stilled and the boat, and they looked into each other's eyes and kissed and kissed.

Beckett concentrated on the side of her neck. Luna moaned and looked up at the stars. "The sky is beautiful tonight."

He kissed her throat and her chin and her lips. "It is."

She said, "You didn't even look."

He said, "You look." While she looked up, he searched her eyes. "There, now I've seen."

He kissed back down her neck to her shoulders and down and pulled up her shirt and fondled there for a moment. She ran her fingers around on the back of his head, holding him close, closer, closest. He rose on his knees over her and pulled his shirt off over his head.

She watched appreciatively as his arms stretched and his chest expanded. Then she raised her arms waiting, so he pulled hers off too. He climbed back on top of her body and ran his hands up and down her side and her front. "I'm sorry about the bandages."

"That's okay."

She ran her hands down his bare back and into the top of his shorts and pushed them down while her tongue flitted inside of his lips, teasing him. He tried to catch her mouth, her lips then groaned. "I want to stay here and play and take my time but I—"

She shoved the back of his shorts down again and teased, "You want me?"

"Yeah," He shook his head, "I can't wait."

She kissed him really slowly looking into his eyes. "Take off my pants."

He yanked at her pants and pulled them to her ankles and barely off one leg. Shimmying his own off, he lowered himself back down.

She bit his lip and said, "Go."

———————————

Later they were still and wrapped around each other. Beckett asked, "Am I crushing you?"

She said, "No, don't move — stay just like this." He kissed her in the soft hair in front of her ear.

Her hands ran softly down his back, up and down, memorizing his form, the hard and soft, his breaths and small vibrations. She held tighter, wanting him still, more, longer. She repeated, "Don't go."

"I'm here." His breath was hot on her neck, she inhaled it in.

Chapter 25

Hours later Beckett's eyes opened suddenly. It would be dawn soon and they were naked in the Zodiac. He had rolled off Luna but still had an arm and a leg across her body. He whispered, "Luna? Wake up."

She started awake, gave a frightened look around, then settled on Beckett's smile. "Hey Beckett."

"Hey. We have to get up, go to the bunk room. There's a bunk there for you."

She said, "I guess staying here isn't acceptable?"

"My pale ass is shining up at the bridge — probably not."

They struggled up in the Zodiac, hunted for their clothes in the dark, and dressed giggling. Then Beckett led her by the hand to the bunks, showing her a bed at the end of the hall. Across from Jeffrey.

He pantomimed where the bathroom was, and returned to his bunk for his grandmother's quilt, unfolded it, and covered her. He knelt beside her bunk and kissed her. "I'll see you in the morning."

She nodded and he walked away.

Luna stared up at the ceiling made of Dr Mag's bunk, three feet above her head. The boat shifted and rocked and the engine rumbled and she was warm and comfortable enough, but also alone. She looked around at the shadows surrounding her. People, sleeping, on the water. Familiar, but also different and she couldn't — she turned to her side and flipped to her other side, then her back and stared at the ceiling some more. She looked at the corners, closer, the ceiling bowing down, she could feel it dropping, pressing. Her heart raced. She pulled the blanket to her mouth and tried to close her —

"Luna?"

She jerked her eyes open. Beckett was kneeling beside her bunk. "I can't sleep," he whispered. "Can you?"

She shook her head.

"You want to go sit on deck chairs?"

She nodded gratefully and followed Beckett back up the stairs.

Chapter 26

The next morning Beckett and Luna greeted them all as they appeared, hung-over, in the galley. Dan was ecstatic that coffee had already been made. He poured a mug and joked, "This is what this ship needs, someone to wake up and make coffee for everyone."

Beckett mumbled, "Your job."

"A man can dream." He appraised Beckett, who was smiling, full dimples showing. "You're grinning like a recently sexed schoolboy, apologies Luna for my bluntness, I guess you had a good night in my Zodiac, Army?"

"I had a good night." Beckett passed Dan the sugar for his coffee and a spoon. "Last I checked that Zodiac belongs to the ship."

Dan grinned. "True that, I just borrow it. When there's a need." Sarah clambered down the stairs. Dan said, "Isn't that right baby? When there's a need?"

"Jeez honey, you talking about sex again? You're incorrigible."

Dan pouted. "Army started it. Look at him, all smiles. He had sex last night. You can see it all over his face, apologies again Luna." Then he pouted. "Why didn't I?"

Sarah gave his shoulder a playful slap, "You were too drunk last night and you know it." She wrapped her arms around his head and he nestled into her chest. She whispered to Luna, "Don't mind him."

Luna said, "Oh I don't mind. Someone had some mind-blowing sex in the Zodiac last night. As my friend Sky would say, 'I reintroduced him to my spectacular awesome.'"

Dan grinned. "Luna, you're the best."

"Us Waterfolk live in pretty close quarters. We're kind of open and blunt about our antics."

Dan said, "See, I learn something new every day."

Captain Aria appeared and everyone stopped laughing, un-entwined their bodies, and tried to act respectable. She chuckled. "At ease people. Got coffee? I've a bit of a headache."

Rebecca and Jeffrey and Dr Mags appeared next. Dan and Beckett passed out mugs for coffee.

Captain Aria said, "Since you're all here — we've had a change of plans. We have a big storm in the area. Lenny turned us south last night and he's been running all night. It seems like we might as well head back to port. We'll be arriving mid-morning tomorrow."

Rebecca's hair stuck up everywhere and her eyes were unfocused. "So can I go back to bed?"

Everyone laughed. Sarah said, "You know that 'headed back to port' means chores. And also you're the one that needs to assign them. You know, as boss."

Rebecca groaned. "Okay. Okay. It was my birthday yesterday." She stuck her tongue out petulantly. "I'll have a list ready by," she looked at her wrist where there wasn't a watch, "a while from now." She dropped her head to the table, moaned, and spoke directly to Beckett and Luna. "You guys are lucky you don't have to drink."

Captain Aria said, "Well, I'm headed back to the bridge, bring my breakfast up when it's ready Dan. I'll send Lenny down before he gets to bed." With that she climbed up the steps.

Dan said, after checking to make sure she had gone, "Fine, I'll make breakfast. Someone has to, I suppose. Sheesh." He hoisted himself up and disappeared in the kitchen, calling out, "We have too much food left, everyone is going to need to eat double time." He reappeared around the corner. "Luna, heads up," He tossed a chocolate bar.

"Yum, thanks Dan." She ripped into it, bit off a corner, and hugged it to her chest.

Sarah moved into the seat beside Rebecca with a pad of paper and a pen and they began planning all the things that needed to be done to close down and relocate the lab and specimens and equipment. After a bit Dan appeared with eggs, bacon, and toast for everyone, and dictated a list to Jeffrey for closing up the kitchen. Beckett was necessary for parts of both, or all, jobs even with bandaged hands. He would be a floater and do whatever needed to be done. Luna was to wash the decks. She seemed excited about that job which made Dan squint his eyes skeptically. "That's not a fun job."

She looked incredulous. "Not fun? It's water, soap — what do I use?"

"A mop. Sponges."

"Mops, sponges, out on deck, on the ocean, with friends, all working together toward a common goal. I can't think of anything *more* fun." She took another bite of chocolate and grinned.

Beckett leaned over and kissed her on the temple.

The day was long. Beckett and Luna passed each other occasionally and kissed or held hands or just sat and leaned on each other, settling into being together. The chores took all day. Beckett asked Luna to help him at one point with tarp folding and like on the Outpost they spread out the tarps held the corners and moved to the middle to gather them together. Unlike on the Outpost, they kissed when they met in the middle and turned the whole thing into a game. Then Beckett disappeared to the galley while Luna organized ropes, but suddenly she appeared in the doorway of the kitchen, her face paler than usual.

"What's up?"

"Nothing." Her eyes flitted around the room.

"You sure?"

Dan looked up from a box he was filling with pots. "She's hungry again, right Luna? Back for some dinner—" He looked at his wrist. "Damn, I've got to cook." He spun around looking for his apron, lost in thought.

Beckett asked quietly, "What's up?"

"Nothing . . ." She focused on the light switch on the wall beside him. "Did you see the big bank of clouds headed this way? It's um — no big deal. I was wondering if you needed help down here?"

Beckett searched her eyes. "Yeah, I was coming to get you. Can you help me with packing the utensils?"

Relief washed over her face. "Sounds perfect."

Dan said, "Again, not a fun job."

Luna stuck out her tongue.

Thirty minutes later everyone else traipsed down to the galley, showing up at once, loud, boisterous, Jeffrey was last, wet. "The rain has arrived."

They slid into all the booths and looked expectantly, half-jokingly at the kitchen door. Dan looked around the door jamb. "Jeez you guys need to eat again? It's going to be awhile before it's ready, so I don't know, play cards or something." An hour later he fed them a big meal he had conjured up of all the rest of the perishables.

Dr Mags said, "I've been dying for veggies and suddenly you have them? You saved them?"

"In case we needed them, now we do."

"As your doctor I would like to go on the record as saying you need your veggies every day. It's a fact, there's no arguing."

"When did you become my doctor, aren't you an animal Doctor? Maybe you're confusing me with a cow." He placed a heaping plate in front of her and kissed her on the cheek playfully. "I kid, you're not just an animal Doctor you're also Beckett's Doctor."

Everyone ate in silence and Rebecca groaned again. "So how did everyone do on their lists? I'm not close to done, but it's raining now, dark, I don't want to do anything. Can we call it a day? I'm wiped."

Sarah said, "You tell me. I can't think, I need sleep."

"I say we call it. We can finish tomorrow morning and then we have the unloading and moving and unpacking. Poop, let's just go to bed."

Dan said, "Wait! He rushed to the kitchen and returned with a heaping plate of cookies, turnovers, and pastries. "Eat! Finish these and then you can sleep. And Jeffrey, I'll need your help after for cleanup again." He pointed at Beckett with a questioning look.

Beckett shook his head.

"Okay, I only need Jeffrey."

Chapter 27

Luna looked pensive. She had been quiet during dinner and now she kept looking at the door Sarah, Rebecca, and Dr Mags all disappeared through headed for their bunks. Beckett said, trying to sound upbeat. "I guess the Zodiac is out of the question."

Luna distractedly said, "Oh yeah, I guess so." The rain was growing louder. The ship beginning to storm-pitch.

"How about we stay here?" He got the deck of cards and flipped through them. "You know how to play war?"

Luna nodded. She was the quietest he had ever seen her. No easy smile or sparkling mood. Beckett took a turn and then Luna. She said, looking at her cards, "It's not even a big storm, nothing I haven't weathered before."

Beckett placed down a card. "I'm sure."

The ship rocked to the right causing Luna to slide into Beckett. "I mean — is it my turn? It's just we Waterfolk have ways of dealing with storms, that make it easier…" she placed a card down matching Beckett's, and they played out a battle sequence that Beckett won. He took all the cards. Luna seemed not to notice. She had five cards left in her hand.

He asked, "Tell me how Waterfolk deal with storms." The ship pitched left and Luna braced her foot to keep from sliding off the seat.

"I don't know, um, we—" He placed a card, she placed a card. "Go bird. That's one thing, try to hunker down and turn off your brain and get through." The boat pitched forward and free fell causing Beckett and Luna to fly up and crash back to the seat. Beckett's stomach lurched. Luna screamed. Dan in the kitchen yelled, "Hey!" and a pile of something crashed.

He sat sideways on the booth, leaned against the wall, and pulled Luna to his chest. "Come here. This is nothing, right? A minor storm. That was just a big wave and Lenny is probably driving." The boat pitched to the left again. Beckett tightened his hold around Luna.

She said, "It surprised me that's all." He peeked at her eyes, they were closed tight. She was curled in his arms.

The boat pitched forward again and in one quick move Luna dove up under the front of Beckett's shirt.

Beckett chuckled down at the big lump on his front that was Luna's head and shoulders. "Better?"

"Much better." Then she said, "I'm sorry I'm stretching out your shirt."

"No worries."

"It's not that I'm scared. It's—"

"I think I'll join you." He pulled his arms in the sleeves and wiggled his head down into the neck of the shirt, stretching it up and out. Yep, his shirt would be ruined, but he was completely okay with that. He whispered, "So how do you 'Go Bird'?"

Luna lifted her chin and looked up at him. The green of his t-shirt shadowed her face. "Kind of like this. You wrap your wings around your head. The hard part is you're supposed to stop thinking."

He asked, "How are you supposed to do that?"

She said, "I never really figured it out."

He said, "Maybe you have to distract your—"

Dan's voice interrupted them as he came around the corner from the kitchen, "Man, that was — um, Army, whatcha doing?"

Beckett said, from inside the shirt. "I'm going bird Dan, what does it look like I'm doing?"

Dan chuckled. The ship pitched right. "I'm not going to be able to get anything done with this maniac driving the ship, so Jeffrey and I are headed to the bunks. Luna do you need anything?"

Luna's face was pressed into Beckett's chest, under the cloth. She said quietly, "I can't think of anything."

"All right birdies, want the lights off?"

Beckett said, "No, keep them on."

Jeffrey came around the corner, putting on his raincoat to make it from the door of the galley to the door of the bunk room. "Want to share my raincoat to the bunk room?"

Beckett said, "I think we'll stay in here tonight."

Dan said, "If you get bored, the cutlery needs to get packed."

After they left, Beckett began to sing, low and slow, not well, but softly.

Luna asked, "Is that the song we danced to on the Outpost?"

"One of them." He continued, "Oooh, sad to say, that is the way, we gotta play…"

Luna said, "I like that, it's nice, can you keep doing that?"

Beckett nodded and kept singing.

Chapter 28

When they woke up the next morning Beckett and Luna were stiff but relieved that the storm was behind them. They made a pot of coffee and took mugs onto the deck to see the sunrise. It was epic.

They leaned on Beckett's favorite railing. He said, "Well, we made it through."

Luna said, "With you it's never making it through, it's living on."

He put his arm around her. "Thank you. I love you."

"I love you too."

A flock of birds flew past the boat, calling their own style of good morning. Beckett and Luna arched their heads back to watch them fly.

"So we have chores today and then we're at Heighton Port, where it sounds like I have more chores, but *after* I'll call my aunts to come pick us up in the truck. Your board should fit, or we'll rent a trailer or something…"

Luna asked, "What about the camps and the settlements?"

"I've been thinking about that. Why do you have to go? You don't, you're coming to my house, so I think we'll skip that part."

"That makes sense."

"Yeah, we have a lot to figure out, but let's just get you home first."

Chapter 29

The activity on the ship was frenetic. They were boxing, piling, organizing, drying down wet equipment, and then packing it up. Beckett and Jeffrey helped everyone in turns. Luna helped Sarah and Rebecca in the lab, talking about life on the sea, answering questions about her life as Waterfolk. Then there was a farewell lunch. They gathered on deck to eat sandwiches.

Sarah asked, "Beckett, Luna, what's next for you? Will you come out with us next trip?"

Luna looked expectantly at Beckett, would they? This was really awesome. And partly familiar. Familiar enough to not be scary, except of course the storms. But if she wanted to live at sea there would be storms. Question was, did she want a sea-life?

She wanted a life with Beckett. That was all she knew.

Beckett answered, "As great as this has been, I don't think the sea is for me. If you guys would do some land animal research I'd be there in a second."

Luna put her head on his shoulder.

Dan shook his head sadly. "Have you learned nothing Army? You're thinking land-based, but it's the oceans, man. You gotta come to terms with the mysterious depths."

"No thank you. And I'll remind you that Navy chefs need land-based farmers for their food."

"True that."

Beckett asked, "What is everyone else doing?"

Rebecca said, "Me and Dan and Sarah share a flat near the university. Sarah and I go to the office starting Monday and Sarah teaches this semester, so we won't be back on the high seas for many months. It's all so boring, am I right Dan?"

He said, "Boring as hell. I hate it. I can't wait to come back out."

Jeffrey shook his head. "I'm going to miss it. Give me boring any day."

Rebecca smiled sadly then continued, "Dr Mags sits in her recliner until we call her up to come with us on another adventure."

"Not true, I have a job. But I do sit in a recliner a lot."

Captain Aria came down and gave everyone a speech about how much the trip had accomplished and how proud they should be about the research they had conducted. And that the H2OPE would be going back out in four months and they were all welcome. As she finished Luna raised her hand.

"How long until port?"

"An hour and a half."

"Mind if I get out and paddle it?"

Dan interrupted, "You plan to race us to shore Nomad?"

Luna smirked. "It would be foolhardy to suggest that I could beat this big ship. No, I mean to paddle alongside it."

Dan laughed.

Captain Aria said, "We'll pull to a stop, let your board down, and see you at port. It was a pleasure meeting you, Luna."

The lunch was finished. The day was calm and clear. The H2OPE slowed. Beckett asked, "You're sure about this?"

Luna answered, "I told you I was going to paddle to meet you at Heighton Port. I promised. I mean to fulfill that promise."

Beckett nodded. "Wait, wear this." He took off the watch and gave it to her.

She said, "You don't need an insurance policy, I'm coming."

"It's not insurance, it's tradition." He helped her latch it to her wrist and turned on the winch to lower Luna's board to the water.

Luna stood at the opening in the railing at the top of the ladder. She swayed back, stepped forward, and leapt out —

Beckett clamped his eyes closed and under his breath said, "Splash," as Luna hit the water with a kabloosh.

Dan leaned beside him, as well as everyone else on the ship, and they watched as Luna deftly climbed on her paddleboard. Dan bellowed, "On your mark, get set, go!"

Luna grinned a big cheeky grin, put her paddle in the water pushed back, and paddled, fast. Dan said, "Now how about that? Do you see this Beckett — your girl-friend is a freaking goddess."

Beckett laughed.

Dan said, "How can you be smiling? You've got to be asking yourself, how does an army guy keep a woman like that happy."

"I don't know. Seriously. How this will work is a mystery I need to figure out. I'm only smiling because of one thing."

"What's that?"

"She's headed in the right direction."

Chapter 30

Luna paddled with sure strokes to the finish line as everyone on deck cheered. She had fallen behind. She knew she would, it was a ship after all, but she was way faster than anyone had expected.

As she paddled up, she kissed both her biceps with a grin and Beckett laughed while Dan pretended to swoon.

Ropes stretched from the boat, across the large square submerged rooftop to the wooden dock, numbered 49. Luna looked at the scene, docks created a maze around submerged and half-submerged rooftops. Boats were lashed and tied everywhere. Sailers and crew bustling around, cranes hoisting, and farther up on shore, people, so many people and buildings and traffic — she looked back down at her paddleboard. She would need to take this in steps. Concentrate on Beckett. The dock. The port city would come later.

Luna lashed her board to the cleat as Beckett called down from the ship, "Welcome to Heighton Port!"

She called up, "I totally let you win."

He said, "Of course, and because Dan's ego is very fragile, I won't tell him."

Dan was leaning over the railing right beside him. "That was epic Luna. I could watch you paddle all day, but I have more work to do, so I'll see you when you and

Beckett come over for dinner, like next week. Sarah says you have to."

Luna leaned on her paddle and beamed up at Beckett. "Want me to come up?"

Beckett glanced around and seemed surprised to see a stack of plastic boxes beside his feet. "Um, don't come up, wait there for a minute, I want to come down and kiss you on shore. I'll get this to its — and um — I'll come down." He spun away and turned back and rested the box on the railing. "Have I told you how epically glad I am that you're here? That we made it?"

She smiled up at him and he smiled down at her, paused, smiling, happy, momentarily, until he remembered the boxes. "I'm finishing this — down in a second."

He turned away for real this time and darted across the decks to the lab.

Chapter 31

Beckett barged in. "I think this is the last of the boxes? I want to run down and meet Luna on shore. We'll come back in a bit to get our things."

Sarah put down the pen. "Oh Beckett, I didn't think about that. This is momentous isn't it, you and Luna on shore together? That's really great." She came around the counter to hug him.

Rebecca walked in. "Are we hugging goodbye already?"

Beckett said, "Not really, I'll be back for my things, but yeah, I guess we are hugging goodbye."

Sarah was misty-eyed. "Beckett's sea maiden is beckoning from the shore, and his hot self with his tattooed arms and dimpled smile plans to rush into her arms and leave us for good."

Rebecca pretended to sob. "Beckett's leaving us?" She shook her head solemnly and held his shoulders. "You were the kind of hot that was epically good to have around, Beckett."

He rolled his eyes, "Guys, you're objectifying me again."

Rebecca said, "I will never have as good looking an army guy to carry my test tubes." She sighed deeply. "You take care of yourself, if you need an ocean biologist to . .

. I don't know, explain the cycle of fish life, give me a call."

"Definitely Rebecca, It's been really good getting to know you all—"

Behind them Jeffrey, then Dr Mags entered the lab and joined the circle hugging Beckett goodbye when Dan shoved through the door. "The police are talking to your girl."

They rushed to the railing. A police boat was at the end of the dock, two police officers stood in the shadows of the ship with Luna between them. Beckett called down, "What's going on?"

The police officer on the left glanced up, then ignored him.

Beckett climbed down the ladder as Luna's voice rose. "— It's mine, it belongs to me!"

On the bottom rung Beckett leapt to the submerged rooftop and splashed across in a run. One of the police officers yanked Luna's paddle from her grip.

Beckett yelled, "Give that back, it belongs to her! What's your name, your badge number?" He leapt to the dock as a police officer moved to block his way.

"I'm officer Capstone, what business have you got here?"

"She's with me."

The policeman shoved him backwards. "She's not with you. She's a Nomad, and she's unregistered."

Beckett stepped to the left. Officer Capstone blocked him, stepping close, his chest bowed out, eyes locked on Beckett's face.

Behind Beckett Luna begged, "Please don't, please." The other police officer brought his heel down on Luna's paddle with force, breaking the handle in half.

Beckett shoved officer Capstone in the chest, hard, and rushed the officer holding the broken paddle. "That's hers, you give it back."

Two more police officers stepped onto the dock, causing Beckett's attention to shift, and without warning Officer Capstone punched Beckett in the stomach.

Luna screamed as Beckett doubled over. He hadn't seen that punch coming. He should have known better.

Officer Capstone swung again, an uppercut aimed for Beckett's nose. When it connected, Beckett's head jerked back with a blinding blast of pain. Blood rushed down the front of his face.

"Beckett!"

Beckett stumbled back three steps. A club swung down on his back, knocking him forward to his knees, and a boot shoved him face down to the wooden planks. His cheek smacked the ground with a thud. His arms were yanked behind and up, and his wrists were bound.

Luna pleaded, "Please, you're hurting him! You're hurting him!"

Beckett was facing right, Luna was on his left. He couldn't see her. He was contorted, pressed face down. She sounded scared. She was begging, and he didn't understand what was going on. None of this made sense. Plus the pain. Shooting pain blasted around his eyes. His forehead ached. His nose stabbed, full, his breathing labored — it all made him feel like he couldn't calm down.

He yelled, "Luna! You okay?" His lips rubbed on the rough hewn wood of the dock, smeared in his blood. "Are you okay?"

———————————

Part Two:

Port

Chapter 32

"Luna, are you okay?"

A voice growled from above his back, "I didn't say you could talk to her."

Luna sobbed. She sounded so desperate that Beckett clamped his eyes shut and yelled, "Fuck! What are you doing to her?"

Dan was on the dock. Speaking to the police, his voice calm and measured.

Beckett had trouble making out Dan's words over the pain and confusion, but he listened, trying to make them out, "—one of our crew. Yes, sir. Of course. No, I didn't know that—"

Beckett yelled, "Dan, what's going on?"

Luna was all sniffles and whimpers. Dan didn't answer.

A police officer said, "—registration at the camps, paperwork and mandatory health evaluations—"

Dan said, "—Captain will vouch for him, will take him back on board—"

Beckett asked, "Dan, what are they saying, Dan?"

The knee on his back grew heavier and more painful. It was hard to breathe.

Dan said loudly, "Can I speak with my crew member?"

The knee raised from Beckett's back. A voice growled, "Don't get up."

A moment later a knee appeared in Beckett's field of vision. "Dan?"

Dan leaned all the way down, face on the dock. Through the blood in Beckett's eyes, Dan looked blurry and tinted red. "Beckett, these officers say that Luna has to be escorted to the camps. I'm talking them into letting you back on the ship and we'll figure the rest out." Dan clapped him on the shoulder.

Beckett nodded, scraping his cheek on the rough wood. "Yes, as long as she's okay." He raised his shoulders to turn his head. At the end of the dock Luna's bare feet were surrounded by the heavy boots of the police.

Luna voice, her face out of his field of vision, said, "Look what you did to him."

A police officer said, "According to the laws of the Unified Mainland you, Nomadic Water Dweller, will be escorted directly to the closest camp for Organization and Resettlement. The paddleboard will be impounded."

Luna said, "You can't do that, it belongs to me! You can't take my things!" She struggled to get out of their grip. One of the police officers laughed.

Luna begged, "Please don't take it."

Beckett listened to Luna's pleading and closed his eyes to try to block all the pain.

Dan whispered, "Stay calm, we'll get this figured out," and rose again to go to Luna's side. She was still crying, asking where they were taking her paddleboard and trying to grab hold of it as two officers carried it down the dock to their boat.

Beckett wondered if he was forgotten until another knee dropped to his back, knocking out his breath, and causing his brain to panic with lack of air. The person attached to that heavy knee yanked Beckett's wallet from his back pocket. From the corner of his eyes Beckett saw his driver's license and his Army ID passed from officer to officer. Then there was quiet. Luna was sniffling. Beckett was held tightly.

Dan asked, "What's happening now, can you release my guy?"

Capstone said, "They're calling in his ID."

Crap. Beckett closed his eyes.

A minute later police boots thundered down the dock. Fast. "Beckett Stanford, you are under arrest for Refusal to Report, Misconduct, and Felony Desertion during Time of Rising Waters."

The pressure on his back increased, pushing him down, shoving his chest and chin into the wood. Capstone's voice said, "Well, well, looks like you're going to jail for a long, long time."

The other officer said, "Not jail, he'll be headed East, to the front. Worse than jail." His voice sounded gleeful.

Luna whimpered, "Beckett?"

He said, "I'm sorry, Luna, I'm so sorry." His cheek was sanded deep in the wood grain.

Police officers jerked him by the arms to a standing position.

He could see everyone now, his face damp with blood, his sight red-stained — Luna across the dock, arms bound, held by two police officers. The rest of the crew watching over the railing. Dan beside Luna, said, "Beckett, we'll come up with something."

The two officers yanked Beckett by the arms so fast he stumbled as he was pulled past Luna.

He caught her eyes, "I'm sorry. I'm coming for you, don't worry, please don't worry. It's going to be okay, stay safe." He was pulled down the dock and away.

Chapter 33

Luna watched Beckett being led down the dock to the boat. "Where are you taking him?"

"Jail. First, we whooped his ass, now we're taking him to jail."

The other officer laughed, "Did you see that gush of blood? That was an epic ass beating." Luna struggled to get free and the officer yanked her to a standstill. "Don't ask for trouble, Nomad, because your ass isn't worth it."

They all laughed.

Dan interrupted, his jaw clenched, "May I speak to the Nomad for a moment?"

An officer sized him up. "Yeah, whatever." He gripped her bound arms tighter.

"I never asked, but um," Dan felt his pockets, and found them empty. "I need your surname, so we can find you in the camps."

Luna said, her voice panicked, "Is he going to be okay? Dan, what's happening — is Beckett okay?"

Dan glanced down the dock toward the police boat as Beckett was shoved on board. "I don't know Luna, but he'll be worse if he can't find you." The officer holding her arms grumbled and yanked her arms. Dan said, "I need your full name."

"Um, Luna Saturniidae."

Dan kept patting around his pockets, he called up to the boat. "Sarah, write down—"

The officer growled, "We don't have time for this." He forced Luna down the dock.

Dan hurried to keep up. "I'm worried about the spelling, use Stanford, okay? Beckett's last name, Luna Stanford. That way—"

Over her shoulder she said, "Yes, yes. Luna Stanford. Dan, you'll find him, please find him?

The policeman gruffly said. "That's enough."

Dan said, "It's not enough, I need her details, so I can—"

"She's Nomad, what do you care? And you better shut up unless you want to go to jail with your deserter friend."

Dan called after her. "When's your birthday?"

Luna craned her neck to look back. "I think it was two-and-a-half weeks ago?"

"So, the fifteenth?"

The policeman to Luna's left shoved her and caused her to stumble. He said, "You know, I'm getting tired of this."

Dan ignored him. "August 15th?"

"Yes," Luna said, "And I'm 19 years old."

Dan called after Luna, "Okay, Luna Stanford, born nineteen years ago on August 15."

She was long down the dock now, calling back over her shoulder. "Do you know where they're taking me?"

"Nope, but it's okay, we're coming to get you."

———————————

The police pushed her onto the deck of a boat. Beckett was sitting there, on a bench, leaned forward, hands cuffed behind his back, blood on his face. She asked, "Beckett, where are they taking—"

An officer shoved her down steep steps. Beckett yelled, "Luna!" as she disappeared into the lower interior deck of the boat.

It was windowless and dark. An officer shoved her into a seat, didn't turn on the lights, growled, "Stay here," and slammed the door. The room was thrown into pitch blackness. A clicking noise told her the door had been locked. And then nothing. Complete nothingness.

It was so black that her breathing echoed in her ears, so loud that she started to panic. Where was she? Where was she going? Was Beckett okay? She dropped her forehead to the table and wrapped her arms around her head, the cuffs binding her wrists were tight, sharp, cutting.

Faint voices came from above, barely distinguishable. She desperately tried to Go Bird.

Chapter 34

Beckett's eyes were wild — looking everywhere, trying to make sense of the situation — what his next move should be. Where was Luna? There were five armed men between Beckett and any place she might be. He'd never find her if fighting armed men was step one. "Where are you taking her?"

A gruff voice said, "Wherever we want, and it's none of your business."

He said, "It is my business, that's my wife."

The officers started laughing like it was all some big joke. One said, "Well you're not big on the decision making, huh? Marrying a Nomad — you could probably fuck her without going to all the trouble. Dumbass."

Beckett's ears turned red. He wanted to kill the guy. "She's my wife — legally you have to tell me where you're taking her."

The guy rounded on Beckett, "Oh I do, do I? You got proof that your deserting-ass married that piece of trash Nomad, or am I supposed to accept your honest word?"

Beckett's jaw clenched and unclenched.

The policeman said, "Yeah, you know what, I'm tired of talking to you so you better shut up."

The boat sped south across the bay. The wind had come up, the water churned, the boat dipped and hopped at breakneck speed. Beckett shut his eyes against the wind. He felt green again, not at all like the kind of guy who could get all heroic, fight a bunch of policemen, rescue a girl, and somehow get to shore. So he sat there with his eyes closed trying to think of a plan but instead thinking about the real probability that he would throw up. Possibly pass out.

After about twenty minutes, the boat pulled to a dock where two more police officers were waiting. Beckett's best guess was that now they numbered about seven. The odds of Beckett's heroic rescue were getting worse and worse. "Cargo?"

"Yep, army deserter." An officer yanked Beckett to standing, shoved him up a ladder and onto the dock.

Beckett asked, "What about the girl? Come on, let me see her, okay? Just a quick—"

One of the officers on the dock asked, "What happened? He got walloped by a board?"

Officer Capstone said, "Resisting arrest. Also he was like that when we found him."

Everyone but Beckett chuckled.

Beckett was shoved and yanked as he was passed from the boat to the dock. He stumbled trying to stand where they wanted, but not doing it quick enough, or smart enough, or possibly short enough, or something. He was taller than everyone there, but the officers made up for the height difference with pure animosity.

Beckett said, "I need one minute to speak to my wife—"

Capstone sneered, "He thinks calling her his wife will make all the rest of us keep our hands off the cheap piece of ocean-paddling ass. But he's not taking into account how hot she is." He laughed heartily as they returned to the boat.

Beckett asked the new officers holding his arms, "What are they going to do to her?"

They force marched him up the dock toward shore. "Nothing, they aren't going to do nothing, because no matter how much they want to make your ass crazy, they aren't going to risk their jobs for a good-for-nothing Nomad girl."

The other said, "You should be worried about where they're taking her."

Beckett asked, "Where are they taking her?"

"The camps, where she belongs."

Chapter 35

Beckett was roughly dragged into the crowded, stuffy, loud, Heighton Port police station, where he was unceremoniously booked by a gruff man who seemed irritated by Beckett's wounded face. As if Beckett had beaten himself on purpose to make everyone uncomfortable. Beckett asked, "What, is my black eye bothering you? The blood on my shirt? That was Officer Capstone. Are you writing it down on my booking papers? Taking note?"

Apparently the gruff man didn't plan to take note.

He was shoved into a jail cell crowded with twelve other inmates. No one talked, they glowered. They glared. He glared back. Or slumped his head against the wall and tried for inconspicuous. Rebounding between furious, want-to-pace-the-room anger, and defeated, want-to-curl-up, fear. Crap, and this morning had seemed so promising.

Chapter 36

He spent the night on a cot made of hard plastic. It was two inches too short. No pillow, a really small blanket. The blanket was fine though because the air was insanely hot. A sweaty, stinky, gross, crowded jail. Beckett hoped the judicial department had fans or else the judges would be total pissed off, sitting on their sweat-covered asses.

The following day, at three o'clock, he was forced to change into a beige, thick, scratchy, questionably clean jumpsuit, then led into a room where Dan was sitting at a table. Beckett dropped into the chair opposite. "Man, I wish you didn't have to see me like this, all criminal like this . . ."

Dan looked at him piercingly. "How ya holding up, Army?"

"Not well. Clearly I'm in some deep shit."

Dan bit his lips, "Yeah, I don't know anyone who deserted that didn't go away for a long, long time."

"I was close to done too. Half a year — because I was such a model soldier."

"That sucks. You could have told us."

"Nothing you could have done. The moment I walked onto that ship I became a deserter."

Dan grinned, "One more reason why you should have gone Navy. I've never been on a boat where I wasn't exactly where I was supposed to be." His expression turned back to serious. "The reason I wasn't here earlier is I've been searching for Luna."

Beckett leaned forward anxiously. "You have? Did you find her?"

"No, not yet."

Beckett ran his hands down his face.

Dan said, "But I will, I'm told it will take between 12-72 hours to get her booked in the system. And then — so I'll keep checking, every few hours, me or Sarah, we'll make them look for her again. Until — but I have to tell you, everyone I've talked to so far has a piss-poor attitude. These are some generally shitty people. You need to get yourself out and get her out, pronto. Luna isn't going to last long there."

Beckett nodded. "True that, but they haven't even offered me a call yet. Will you call my aunt, tell her I need a lawyer?"

Dan wrote down the number and tucked it into his wallet, then stood up. "All right, I'll see you tomorrow Beckett."

"You don't have to, I'm sure you've got things to do. . ."

"I'm Navy, stuck on shore leave, which is almost as ridiculous as Army deserting to the sea. I'm useless. Your hopeless cause is giving me something to do besides washing aquariums for Sarah. I hate washing aquariums. The only good part about washing aquariums is the water hose."

Beckett nodded. "Thanks man."

"Besides you're like the little brother I never had."

Beckett chuckled.

Dan said, "But then again, I do like Luna a lot more. She's like the little sister I never had, which would make you more like my brother-in-law. Yeah, that seems kind of fitting, that way I can roll my eyes whenever I talk about the army guy that's in jail and in love with my little sis." Dan grinned and left.

And Beckett was shoved back to his cell.

Chapter 37

Luna was delivered to the northernmost docks by the leering, disgusting, stiff-neck, jerk policemen. The worst thing that had happened was one grabbed her ass, pulled her close, scared the breath out of her. But she was grateful nothing worse had happened. Grateful and pissed that she needed to be grateful. Furious that they had scared her like that.

It was as if she was under arrest, but all she had done was come ashore. And the way they beat Beckett. She wanted to kill them. She needed to know if he was okay.

A dumpy woman in a uniform with a badge that said, "Sue James, Guard," led her by her elbow down the docks and shoved her into the open maw of a cavernous warehouse. Luna was told to stand in line behind eight other Waterfolk women. The woman directly in front of Luna had long dark hair and was older, older than Luna's mother had been when she —

Luna whispered, "Do you understand what's happening?"

One of the guards shushed Luna aggressively. The woman answered with a quick shake of her head.

So she quieted. Three scowling female guards called the first woman forward. They made her undress and then they sprayed her with a hose and scrubbed her body with brushes. She cried. Luna tried hard not to watch, but by the end, the anguish of the woman being bathed, the fear of the other women in line, it was all too much — tears rolled down Luna's face and the lump in her throat wouldn't swallow down.

She wanted to do something brave, like shove everyone aside, and make a break for it, but she had nothing — no money, no food, not even an idea where she was. And maybe she would be in worse trouble if she attempted to run and got caught.

And why she was in trouble? None of this made sense.

After she was showered, a surly woman shoved what looked like a pillowcase into her arms. Luna unfolded it to see something that was a cross between a robe and a dress. Velcro cinched the waist. She put it on, ran her fingers through her hair, and shuffled to the opposite end of the warehouse where the other women, all dressed in the same sack dresses, waited by a door. Her fear rose. She needed someone to comfort her, maybe a smile or a kind word, but all the other women looked so frightened they wouldn't meet her eyes.

A few minutes later a guard gestured with a grunt that they should follow him through a tented tunnel, across a parking lot, to, finally, a chain-link fenced area. The fence was at least ten feet tall. It had barbed wire curled around on top. The enclosure like a pen. A big pen. For animals. Luna's stomach lurched. A woman said, "What the hell is this place?"

Hundreds of Waterfolk gathered near the door as the guard stuck a key into the padlock and yanked at it with irritation.. One man asked, "When are our administration hearings? When will our lawyers arrive?" More voices rose, asking the same questions, pushing forward to the door, scaring Luna, making her want to duck down and refuse to go in, but she was given no choice. She was shoved from behind, holding her arms like a shield, and forced into the clamoring crowd.

Behind her the guard grunted, "I told you yesterday, the paperwork is coming when it's ready." The door slammed, the lock clicked, and the guard stomped away.

A man yelled toward his back, "That was what you said yesterday; I demand you tell me when our date of release will be!"

The guard raised his hand dismissively and continued walking.

The crowd around the door dispersed and Luna was left standing alone. Inside a locked pen. Sure she was surrounded by fellow Waterfolk, but these weren't the Waterfolk of the high seas, these were Former Waterfolk, lost, landed, dry, beaten down, and depressed. They weren't happy to see her or welcoming or even seeming to notice she was there.

Worst part? She was still standing on the cement of the parking lot, but a foot further, most of the pen, it was all mud.

What had been the purpose of that humiliating shower to go into a pen with a mud floor? Luna was shocked. Horrified. And where was Beckett — where was anyone who could help her?

Chapter 38

The next day Beckett had another visit from Dan.

"I found her. She's at the camps."

"Oh, thank god." Beckett dropped his head to his hands. "Jeez, man, okay what do we—"

"There's a problem though. Sarah and I can't get past the nimrod at the front desk. He's a total tool — shuffled through paperwork, finally admitted she was there — she was logged in this morning. But then informed me that the camp is off limits to visitors. Can you believe it? I was thinking I could sneak through, but Sarah is worried I'd get Luna in trouble, you know?"

Beckett pressed his thumb to his lips, "Yes, Sarah is probably right. Thank you though. I appreciate it."

"We have to come up with a plan, she can't stay there. We need an endgame."

"Yeah, you're — what was it like? What was the vibe? It's like she's been arrested, but for what? I don't get it."

"I don't know. I've seen photos of the camps and they seem awful, but I think they're just a way station. . ."

Beckett nodded. "Just temporary, that's what I think too." He ran his hand up and down on his scalp. "We have to check every day until they're ready to move her. Where do they move them?"

Dan said, "I've been asking about that. It's supposed to be a settlement of some kind, but no one knows where or when. The idea sounded so planned when I heard about it on the news, but now that I'm investigating, no one seems to understand the actual plan."

Beckett whistled. "This sucks — did you get our things off the ship?"

"Yes, they're at our place."

"Then you've got my keys, mind getting my motorcycle? You can park it in long term parking, I have money. It looks like I'll be here for a while."

Dan grinned, "Awesome! Sarah won't let me ride motorcycles, but as a favor, how can she refuse?"

Beckett jokingly groaned, "You know how to drive her, right? Promise you won't hurt her?"

"Promise."

"Look man, I appreciate all of this. I don't know what I would do without your help."

"'Course you do, and of course I am, because you're dating my favorite little sister. So I have to. Even though you're an Army guy and she's dating you against my years and years of brotherly advice."

Beckett chuckled, "You could tell her, but Luna just wouldn't listen."

Dan shook his head slowly, "I kept saying, 'Sis, Army battles against the water, Navy floats on top of the water, which one you want to spend your life with?' But would she listen?"

"She did not. I'm glad she didn't." Beckett sighed. "Navy has its own battles though."

"True, but I prefer those to battling man any day."

"I've been lucky so far, sandbags."

Dan nodded sadly. "Yes, you've had an epic lucky streak so far, the Outpost didn't collapse, you found Luna twice, maybe it will get you out of heading East to the front."

"Maybe—but I can't see how. How's Jeffrey doing?"

"He's booking out tomorrow. Three years. We have a going away dinner tonight but it won't be very festive. Not like on the ship. Man, I want to go back out."

They sat quiet for a second and Dan added, "Dr Mags said she would try to get in to see her tomorrow. Maybe as a doctor she can—"

"Yeah, that would be really good. And tell Jeffrey bye from me, I look forward to seeing him again."

"I will man. Not in the East though, here in Heighton Port or onboard the H2OPE."

"Yeah." Beckett stared off into space for a second. "Do you think she'll hate me for this? I made her come to shore. I told her it would be okay."

"She forgave you for the dart in her ass, so probably."

Beckett nodded and stood to go back to his cell. This sucked. He was asking too much of people, but he still needed more. It had been days. He had involved all these people and still, all he knew was Luna was alive. Nothing more.

It was so frustrating that he needed to go sit in his cell on a cold hard bench and press his hands to his eyes.

Chapter 39

Another day passed when nothing happened. Beckett asked every guard who walked by, "When will I get a lawyer?"

He was either cursed at or ignored. He was in a holding cell, but holding for what?

Finally, on the third day, during visiting hours, it wasn't Dan sitting at the table, it was Aunt Chickadee and her lawyer Roscoe. A wave of relief washed over Beckett.

Chickadee jumped from her chair, and rushed Beckett, hugging, rocking, and holding him tight in her soft fluffiness, as if she'd never let him go. Her green Mohawk was combed down, her shirt printed with big bright flowers, her ears sported five rings each, and her arms were sleeved with tattoos.

Chickadee put her hands up on his cheeks. "Beckie, your face, did they do that to your face?"

He nodded.

"You have blood all over your shirt, poor boy."

Roscoe stuck out his hand to shake Beckett's, he asked, "Were you resisting?"

"They beat me before they were arresting me."

Roscoe said, "Now see, that there is where they lose their high ground."

Chickadee asked, "Are they feeding you?"

Beckett said, "Enough."

"Well, we aren't allowed to be here for long, so Roscoe better get to it." She plopped down to her chair, chins wiggling. Beckett was psyched that Roscoe was there. He hadn't wanted to get his hopes up, had resigned himself to whoever the city would offer him as a lawyer, but now — Roscoe was crazy smart. Never-lost-a-case smart.

The kind of smart that could get Beckett out of here. He hoped.

Plus Roscoe grew up with Chickadee and was one of her biggest fans, so she called him "My Lawyer" because he would do whatever she wanted, whenever she asked. Everything except put on a suit. He was a jeans guy. Often saying, "That way when I argue my case brilliantly they never see me coming."

Roscoe sat down slowly, leaned back in his chair, and leveled his gaze, "Chickadee didn't relay a lot of the details. You've deserted your post?"

Beckett's jaw clenched. "Yes, I guess that's what it looks like — I was allowed a weekend to go home, instead I went to search for a lost friend. I was supposed to report back on the twenty-third. But I was still on board a ship, so um, I had extenuating circumstances."

Roscoe nodded slowly, peering at Beckett long after Beckett stopped speaking. He pulled a stack of papers up and flipped through them. "It looks like you'll be serving five more years, in the East."

"I can't do five years. I was so close to done." Beckett rubbed up and down on his face and up and around and through his now longer and scruffier hair. "Aargh." He leaned back, then leaned forward again. "I volunteered to go to the Outpost, that was supposed to get me a choice of wherever I wanted to go. That was the deal. Also, I

122

planned to report, as soon as I came into Heighton Port. Those fucking jerks arrested me before I had a chance."

Roscoe nodded slowly again and blinked a few times.

Chickadee looked from Roscoe to Beckett and back to Roscoe. "You can handle this right? I mean, he didn't hurt anyone, you've got this, right?"

Roscoe took a moment to arrange his face into deeply confident sneer. "Oh, yes, we've got this."

Beckett asked, "We do?"

Roscoe deposited the papers back into his briefcase and clicked his briefcase closed. "I don't want to make it sound too easy. You'll have some more time added, but I'm sure your battalion needs you. It will simply take some negotiating."

He rose. "You'll have to be careful though, no more screwing up. This one is going to be on your permanent record." He glanced around to see if he left anything on the table and added, "Yep. It will."

Beckett was so surprised at Roscoe's assurances, that he hadn't noticed their meeting was over. He had forgotten to mention Luna. "I also need your help for my friend — an, um, Nomad.

Roscoe's eyes narrowed. He sucked in his lips and made a popping noise and sat back down.

Chickadee clapped her hands merrily, "Is this the girl you told me about? The one you went searching for?"

Beckett nodded. "I found her — in the whole ocean — I found her."

Chickadee said, "That means something."

"I think so too. I was going to bring her home. She — she got detained when I was arrested." Beckett ran his hands though his hair again. "She's at the camps, but Dan hasn't been able to see her yet."

Roscoe raised his eyebrows. "Well now, that's a bigger problem."

"How? She hasn't done anything wrong. I get why I'm in jail, she was simply standing on a dock."

Roscoe and Chickadee exchanged a look. She explained, "The camps are overcrowded and way more complicated than anyone thought. In the beginning they were going to build settlements, but now with the water rising the political will just isn't in settling the nomads anymore."

"Are you saying those people are sitting there in camps waiting for nothing?"

"No one knows what to do with them."

Beckett dropped his hands to the table in front of him, palms up, jaw dropped, dismayed. "I sent people there. I told them to go to the camps. I read them an edict, assured them they'd be safe. . ."

"They aren't safe anymore—"

"But they should let them go — give them back their paddleboards and let them go!"

Chickadee said, "They should, dear, of course."

Roscoe folded his hands carefully and seemed to be choosing his words. "It's not as simple as that when you have a tiny little brain, and the bureaucrats running the Nomadic Water People Policy have very small brains. I have heard it said that the government of the American Unified Mainland can't possibly let the Nomads go because the Administration feels responsible for them. I have also heard it said that they no longer wish to feed them. So there you go."

Beckett looked at him incredulously. "Not feed them — I have to get Luna out of there. Can you help me?"

Roscoe nodded slowly, not in agreement but as if to acknowledge hearing the question, and that he was mulling it over.

He took so long that Beckett turned to Chickadee. "I love her. I want her to live with us. I promised her. She doesn't have anyone — her whole family is gone, and she's all alone. I promised her that I would give her a home."

Chickadee's eyes filled with tears. "Oh Beckie, is she wonderful? I mean she must be if you love her so much, but is she amazing? Is she the punchline to your life's joke?"

Beckett nodded. "Definitely, someday, nothing feels very funny right now."

Chickadee clapped her hands on her thighs, "That's all I need to hear. Roscoe, let's go get the girl." She acted like she was jumping up from her chair.

Roscoe shook his head slowly, "Now Chickadee, it's not going to be as easy as all that." Chickadee rolled her eyes and slumped back down to her seat. He said, "She's a Nomad. I'll have to research precedence, this will require some studying."

Chickadee said, "Well, first, I'm going to march into the camps and demand her. As her Aunt Chickadee. I'm going to demand they release her to me."

Roscoe watched her speak, nodding slowly. "We can try that." He stood with his briefcase.

Chickadee said, "Beckie, what's her name?"

Beckett said, "Her real name is Luna Saturniidae. But Dan said she's listed as Luna Stanford. And before you go crazy, no I didn't get married without you, that's so I can find her easily, get her released with less paperwork."

Chickadee laughed, "I would've killed you, that's true. But also, see, she's got our last name — me and Roscoe are just going to go get her."

Beckett blew out a big gust of air. "Chickadee, thank you."

"If you love her, she's family, and it's time for her to come home."

Chapter 40

Luna had made some friends. Especially once the Waterfolk realized that her family name was Saturniidae. There had been whispering and sad long looks, then a meeting was called after which a family group, the Celastrinas, had taken her into their fold. Luna had never met them or even heard of them, which suddenly made the world seem really too, too big.

They had a niece, Charm, who was a little older than Luna and was okay to talk to, but she supposed the real reason they adopted her was because they had a son, Springer, who was seventeen.

They probably hoped Luna would be a good match.

Springer was goofy and young and barely able to speak two words to her. Some of the time it was funny, but it was also terrifying, that this might be it. That Beckett might never come for her. That he might be gone and this, this pen, this family of strangers, this ankle deep mud, this simpering teen boy, might be her life from now on.

She was sitting with Springer and Charm, in their matching cage clothes, discussing the dampness, the mud, and then they had segued into the bigger conversation — how long they had been there, when would they get to leave — then they circled back to the complaints, because that bigger conversation was too difficult, so completely out of their control, that it couldn't be discussed for long without really freaking everyone out.

Luna had been locked up there for three nights already. Three uncomfortable nights, with thin blankets on the ground. No one slept well, and these were Waterfolk, they were used to the light sleep of the ocean. But the deep ocean was a known. This was awful, the fearful sleep of the unknown.

So far Luna's days had been dry, but she read the sky, rain was eminent. As the wind rose, they moved to the far end under the tree cover. They wrapped in blankets and huddled. It was already very muddy there. The mud was starting to really piss her off.

All they needed to do was break out of here and run for it, in the direction of the ocean. But they also needed their paddleboards and didn't have a clue where they were stored. And not everyone could climb over the fence. But really who was Luna kidding that barbed wire made it dangerous for anyone to try.

This was what Springer and Charm and Luna were discussing — how a human would get through barbed wire at the top of a tall fence, when a commotion happened. Some lady with a shock of green hair and colorfully floral shirt, was waddling down the slope from the administration offices to the pen, yelling about something and gesturing wildly. She was followed by a tall man jogging, his briefcase swinging as he tried to keep up.

A few men left the huddle to meet her at the door, but then one rushed back, "She's carrying on about a Luna, but insists the last name is Stanford, is she someone you know?"

Luna dazedly said, "Oh! Maybe?"

She walked across the pen to the door followed by Springer and Charm and the other curious Waterfolk who were willing to risk the wet because it had begun to sprinkle a bit.

The woman panted, "Are you Luna dear — Luna Saturnidodod um, Stanford — or something?"

Luna said, "Yes, that's me?"

"Oh thank heavens, we found you! Oh dear — I'm Aunt Chickadee, Beckie sent me." She wiped her eyes on the hem of her t-shirt exposing a bunch of doughy midflesh. "We found you — oh, you're such a beauty." Aunt Chickadee hooked her fingers through the fence. "Come here for a second, dear."

It was odd to be so comfortably addressed by this complete stranger, not unlike waking up in that tent with Sky staring at her, but somehow Luna convinced her feet to move forward.

Chickadee explained again, "Beckett sent us, Dear."

"Is he okay?"

"Yes he's fine, he's in jail, but he's fine. My lawyer, Roscoe," she gestured toward the tall man standing beside her, "says he can get him out in a few days."

Luna looked at the ground. "Good." It was good news. It just seemed very separate from her own ordeal — standing ankle deep in mud in the sprinkling rain, locked up, with no idea why.

Chickadee asked, "Do you have food, dear? Do you have water?"

A lump rose in Luna's throat, "There's food, but there's a baby — a woman is breastfeeding and a child who's sick —" The tears came, they spilled over and streamed down her face.

Chickadee clutched the fence tighter. "Oh dear, dear, dear, dear, Roscoe are you hearing this?"

Roscoe nodded slowly. He stepped back judging the length and width of the pen.

Chickadee said, "You stay put dear, Aunt Chickadee is going to get you released, okay?"

Luna nodded sniveling.

Chickadee stalked up the hill to the building. "Roscoe, follow me!"

Chapter 41

A short time later Chickadee hustled back down the hill, with Roscoe again jogging just behind. She began talking loudly before she was within earshot, ". . . not go as expected — those people are absolute asses."

She grabbed the fence when she reached it. "They won't release you dear, into my care, but don't you worry—" She unlatched her belt, feeding the tail of it through the fence. "Don't you worry one bit dear, Aunt Chickadee has this all under control."

Roscoe stood behind Chickadee with a bemused twitch at the edge of his lips.

After Chickadee latched her belt through the chain link, she bellowed, "I am not leaving, not from this spot, not until — is it okay dear if I call you Luna Stanford?"

Luna nodded, "It's what I put on the paperwork."

"Good." Chickadee raised her voice again. "Not until Luna Stanford and—" Chickadee counted heads for a moment, but gave up and yelled, "and everybody gets to leave. I will not leave."

She yelled louder, "And I have friends!"

In a quieter voice she said, "You'll of course begin filing forms or whatever it is you do, won't you Roscoe?"

His bemused look was growing. "As soon as I finish the paperwork for Beckett, I'll begin this case, but in the meantime, you'll be living here Chickadee?"

She bellowed, "You heard me. I'm staying here, right here, until those asses let my Beckie's Luna go home with me. I will not be moved."

She lowered her voice again. "Roscoe, I will need a chair."

She glanced around, "Also a longer chain. Tell Dillybear that we have a regular ol' sit-in happening. I need her to load a truck with fruit and veggies and bring it, pronto." She asked Luna, "Is there anything else you might need dear?"

"We need toilet paper in the bathroom."

Chickadee blinked a couple of times then bellowed, "Roscoe you tell them we are filing so many forms that they will rue this day. You tell them that my partner is coming with a truckload of toilet paper, as well as pads and tampons for these women, and if she makes it here before toilet paper has been installed in the bathrooms I am going to have a hissy fit so big they will never recover. They will all die penniless and frightened. You tell them that."

Roscoe nodded now a full blown smile across his face. "Anything else?"

"Call Peter, tell him to assemble the boys, there is an action afoot."

Roscoe asked, "Luna, will you be hiring me as your attorney?"

Luna stared blankly at Chickadee and Roscoe, "Um, I don't have any money, I don't—"

Chickadee said, "It's a formality dear, Roscoe doesn't need money, he practices law as sport. Isn't that right Roscoe?"

Roscoe nodded slowly. "It's more of a hobby."

Chickadee said, "A hobby my ass, you like to make people squirm." She turned to Luna, "but if you want him to act on your behalf, you have to say you hire him. So he can."

Luna said, "Oh okay, I hire you."

Roscoe said, "Perfect, Luna Stanford, I'm going to go get started getting you out of here." He hiked back up the hill to the offices.

Chickadee straightened her t-shirt, "Looks like we'll be here together for a while. But don't you worry, from here on out this will be fun." She raised her voice, and bellowed, "Especially once the film crew shows up!"

Luna smiled, her first smile since she had smiled up at Beckett from the dock days before. "A film crew?"

"Oh yes, my friend Peter is a camera man. And he's going to bring some friends to keep us company while we wait for Roscoe to work his magic."

"All of this for me?"

Chickadee smiled. "Of course dear Luna, our Beckie thinks the world of you, so that's that." She crossed her arms and shifted her weight a few times. She sighed. "I'm going to be without a chair for a bit, so to keep my mind off my feet, why don't you tell me about when you met."

And so Luna began the story.

Chapter 42

Luna's days grew busy. Chickadee remained chained to the fence, alongside two of her close male friends, Peter and Aaron, who were there as back up, for bathroom breaks when necessary. They — Peter, Aaron, and Chickadee — had apparently done this before, they had plans, were organized, and talked a lot about past "actions." The encampment around Chickadee grew.

Camp chairs with umbrellas were assembled in a circle beside coolers full of food. Beckett's Aunt Dilly arrived with a truckload of fruits and vegetables from their farm community. She drove the truck right up to the fence, then she and Chickadee lead the rest in banging with sticks, making a riotous ruckus, until a guard arrived to unlock the gate. They passed food into the pen. It wasn't enough for everyone, but every child and the breastfeeding mother got something, Luna was happy about that.

Dilly also brought toilet paper and tampons and pads, beating the city's supplies, and outraging Chickadee, who bellowed and carried on and on about it. "Roscoe you'll be filing about this — you see, don't you? These people are being treated like animals, you see this, don't you?"

Roscoe nodded, said, "I do indeed see," and tromped off back to an office to discuss the matter.

More people showed up, including, as Chickadee had promised, a film crew. Luna acted as mediator between the Waterfolk and everyone camped outside the fence.

A group of students with clipboards arrived, invited by Roscoe, to interview the Waterfolk through the links. They asked for their full name, age, family, and how long they had been in the camp. Also, what their typical nutritional load had been before the camp and since. Some of the particularly interesting interviews were filmed. Roscoe asked for copies of everything.

On the third night, after the bustle of talking, bellowing, interviewing, and generally acting as hostess of the whole place all day, Chickadee was exhausted. She reclined in her camp chair, feet up on a cooler, a bag of popcorn balanced on her bosom. She stuffed a handful of popcorn into her mouth, wiped her buttery fingers on a napkin and grinned. "These asses better figure something out soon, I do not want to have to go on a hunger strike."

Luna sat cross-legged on the other side of the fence, marveling at Chickadee's commitment. None of this was her trouble at all, yet here she was. "Thank you."

Chickadee said, "You don't have to thank me dear, for any of this — this is human decency is what this is." She raised her voice, "Am I right Peter — Human decency!"

Peter said, "You're right Chickadee, as always."

Luna chuckled. She was so grateful. Even if Chickadee didn't want her to say it. Luna was used to people who went with the flow — Chickadee was a blockade, a course changer, a power house. She didn't do anything by consensus. She demanded your compliance, then she called you baby and love and sweetly smiled, and you had to do what she wanted. She had set her mind to this and believed she was right and that this was important and somehow, through sheer force of personality, everyone went along with it. And she was on Luna's side.

That was a nice change. To have someone on her side.

Actually many someones. Roscoe was working tirelessly. Dilly, who was almost an exact opposite of Chickadee, thin and spiky, poetical and demure, had thrown her all into Luna's cause, simply because Chickadee had said it was important. They seemed to trust each other in everything.

Luna said, "I mean thank you for something else beyond the human decency."

Chickadee smiled, popped another handful of popcorn in her mouth, and chewed. "Luna, I really haven't done anything for you in this short time that requires a thank you."

Luna said, "Except for the fact that you were so accepting of me. Like I am. Caged. Alone. Absolutely nothing to my name — and it's not even my name — it's Beckett's name." Luna looked at the fence separating them, the spiraling spiked wires above and the mud below. "You just met me and I just met Beckett. By my calculations he and I have been together a few days in the course of a few weeks, and if you think about it, honestly, I've been nothing but trouble for him. And you. But somehow you're still here, and you're being so nice, even though I don't deserve it. If Beckett hadn't come searching for me, he wouldn't be in trouble right now."

Chickadee watched her as she spoke, her brows furrowed. "Dearest one, did Beckie tell you about his childhood?"

Luna shook her head.

Chickadee said, "Well, It's not my place to. And maybe Beckett never tells you, because sometimes we need to share what is before us, instead of dwelling in the past. It's his right to tell or not, but I will say this — it was the kind of childhood that could break a person. But it didn't. Beckett came out of it, let's say, awesome. I'm his aunt though, I might be partial." She chuckled and wiped her fingers on the napkin that was now a wad of very butter-slimed paper. "Beckie deserves a big love story — the kind that follows the stars and jumps from buildings and loses its mind under the constellations. He deserves the kind of story that makes you breathless when you hear about it. And when you told me the story the other night, about how you met, and how you fell in love, I got a little breathless at the thought. That's the kind of love story he deserves. And so I might not know you very well," she shifted her ample bottom in the camp chair, "but I trust you because you're the woman at the other side of that story."

Chickadee dropped the empty bag of popcorn beside her chair. "If you hadn't found Beckett what would have happened to you?"

Luna sifted some pebbles near her knee. "I'm not sure."

Chickadee looked at her more piercingly. "I think you do know."

"Yeah, I know, but I guess I don't want to dwell on the past but look at the future."

Chickadee smiled. "Of course dear. I'm not going to say it will be easy, but I'm glad you're here."

Luna asked, "Is Beckett okay?"

"I'm not going to lie to you, the prison is not allowing visitors. His case is dire. But Roscoe's working it, and he's a genius. In the meantime, Beckett is sitting tight, waiting to be let out. Like you. Oh, we'll have fun, all of us, when you're both home. And if you think I'm a hoot, wait until you see Dilly when she's preparing some fabulistic spoken word for one of our parties."

"How did you two meet?"

Chickadee closed her eyes and folded her hands on her rounded belly. "It was in a Political Science class in college. I took one look at her and — ka-pow! So when I walked down the aisle I made sure to bump her desk and sent her pencil cascading to the floor. Back then I was already sporting ample hips, so it was easy to do, and when I looked behind me, to see if she noticed, her eyebrow was arched like Cleopatra, and she had a smile on the edge of her lips. She said, 'Would you like to go get a cup of tea with me after class?' Which everyone knows means fall in love with me, so I did. I fell in love."

Chickadee opened one eye and looked at Luna, "It's okay if that didn't make you breathless, the good stuff came later. Someday I'll tell you about it, but now I need some sleep."

Luna nodded. "You ought to get some, the rain will be here mid-morning."

Chickadee opened her eyes. "Rain? But there's no roof on this pen!" She grunted up out of her chair. "This is unconscionable!"

She bellowed toward the building, "I want tarps. Enough tarps for the entire pen, by morning, or my lawyer Roscoe will sue you until I'm sitting under a roof made of your cash!"

Chapter 43

A few days later Beckett was led to his arraignment hearing. Roscoe was waiting for him wearing worn out, faded jeans and a green shirt, not at all lawyer attire. The exact opposite of the clothes he should be wearing. Beckett was wearing his dirty-beige prison-pantsuit. He looked like a criminal, and his lawyer looked like an amateur. Beckett took a deep breath and tried to trust Roscoe's instincts.

Beckett had so many questions that his head hurt. He had just been waiting, no visitors, lonely, confused, staring at the walls, it wasn't even until this morning that he was told there would be a hearing. Today, no preparation. No rehearsal. Roscoe greeted him and simply said, "When we get in here I'll do the speaking. You try to look reformed and apologetic. No arguing."

Beckett chewed his lip and wondered what he might have to argue about. As far as he could tell this was done; he was headed East, the front lines, as bleak an ending to his short life as he could imagine.

Roscoe shoved the door open. "But smile a little or you'll look like an ax murderer and then there's nothing I can do." And Beckett realized that Roscoe was joking, and his confusion deepened.

Beckett scanned for Luna. He didn't expect her, but he hoped. She wasn't there. Dan was though, about eight rows back. He was sitting between Sarah and Rebecca. Dr Mags was there and even Captain Aria. That sucked. He didn't like wearing prisoner garb in front of Captain Aria. That really, really sucked. They all waved. Beckett nodded in return.

The room was crowded. People sat in rows of folding chairs nervously watching the judge, a silver-haired man sitting at the front of the room. He looked dignified, his spine straight, his hair on point, even though the temperature in the room was extremely elevated, and his table and chair were the folding kind. Temporary. The furniture worried Beckett, it didn't seem like the kind of furniture his case required.

Beckett wiped at his sweaty forehead with the back of his arm, looked down at his filthy clothes, and glanced again at Roscoe's jeans. He reminded himself about a time two years ago when Roscoe had won a case against the company that was stealing water from the local aquifer. He had been wearing jeans. He had won all of Beckett's cases through the years, always in jeans. Though this case seemed more dire, extreme enough to require a bit more dignity.

A young man stood in front of the judge's table, looking confused and frightened. The judge's expression was stern, worn out, and unhelpful. The young man's lawyer was wearing a suit. *Crap.*

Roscoe leaned in. "Chickadee wishes she could be here, but she's tied up at the moment — with your friend Luna."

"Oh, um, okay, good, good."

Beckett followed Roscoe to the side and as he leaned on the slightly cool cinderblock wall, Roscoe whispered, "I know the judge."

Beckett said, "Really? Is that good?"

Roscoe shook his head and Beckett couldn't tell if he meant that wasn't good, or if he meant Beckett should be quiet.

So Beckett quietly watched people approach the front table and speak in hushed tones about their cases. He watched them looking distressed after the judge spoke. One woman cried. The judge seemed to enjoy making people suffer.

After about an hour Beckett's name was called by a bailiff who gestured for them to approach the table. Roscoe pulled a stack of papers from his briefcase. The judge didn't bother to look up, instead lifting pages, reading notes, and acting as if their presence at his table was an annoyance. Beckett had been standing there for about thirty seconds and already felt like that was too much. Perhaps he should bow and back away, possibly come back when the judge was in a better mood. . .

The judge huffed and allowed the last page to drift back down. Then his gaze traveled up Roscoe's jeans, to his lack of belt, past his frayed belt loops, to his wrinkled shirt, and finally, up to his face. He gasped, "Roscoe Gentry, is that you?"

"The one and the same."

"Are you practicing law again?"

Roscoe said, "When the world requires it."

"Well imagine that. This fellow, um," the judge looked down at the paperwork, "Beckett Stanford — this is your case? Desertion. Isn't this beneath you? This decision is simple — time East, at the front. There's precedence."

Roscoe nodded and responded slowly, "That's all true, but, well, Beckett is unprecedented. He comes from a good family near me, and he volunteered to live on an Outpost for six months."

The judge looked at Beckett for the first time. "You volunteered?"

"Yes sir."

There was a pause while the judge peered up into Beckett's face, and Beckett tried to look respectable and civilized, despite the drip of sweat sliding down his cheek.

Roscoe added, "He came back early — the Outpost was unstable, and there were family issues to deal with. A death in the family. A friend who went missing. He missed his report back time, but was headed there when he was picked up by the police."

The judge flipped through the paperwork again, located a page and scanned. "Any trouble during the arrest? It doesn't say here, but he has injuries."

"He did not resist arrest."

"I see. So what are you proposing, Roscoe?"

"That he be allowed to resume his duties with his battalion. They need him, especially with the water rising. He can finish out his time."

The judge nodded vaguely. "You still living in Charlesville?"

"I am, on my family's farm. We have an epic crop of okra this year."

"I remember your grandmother's cookies like it was yesterday."

"She's long gone, but the recipe lives on. The secret is in the butter. Plus the pecans have to be chopped to just the right size."

Beckett held his breath as the judge looked back down at the papers. "I guess that's all I need."

He gestured to a clerk who bustled up to receive the paperwork. "Mark this one sentenced." He glanced at Beckett, "What about your bandaged hands, are you able to perform your duties?"

"My doctor will remove the bandages today."

"Okay, then he'll report back to his battalion, a six month tour."

Beckett let the air out with a rush.

Roscoe shuffled the papers into his briefcase and without saying a word turned for the door. Beckett followed. He didn't speak, celebrate, show any emotion, worried that any sign of relief might cause the judge to change his mind.

As soon as they got to the hall Roscoe checked his watch. "That's done. The bus back to your battalion leaves in three hours."

Dan rushed from the hearing room and swept Beckett into a hug. "Nicely done, Army!" He was followed by Sarah, hugging Beckett tearfully. She said, "We were so worried about you, Dan was practically frantic."

Dan laughed and joked, "I don't know, frantic? But in a cool way, right? Like, frantically coolly worried about Beckett."

Beckett laughed and threw his arm out and hugged Dan again, and Rebecca smiling happily hugged them both, and Dr Mags and Captain Aria beamed and clapped him on the back with congratulations and excitement. Beckett said, "That was — phew. But now I only have three hours to get released and see Luna."

Dan said, "Sarah and I will wait for you."

Chapter 44

Getting released took an excruciatingly long time. The prison doctor gave Beckett a cursory check up and removed his bandages. His hands were scarred, pale and wrinkled. They didn't look like the kind of hands that should be heading out to labor, slinging sandbags against a rising tide. They were desk job hands, yet Beckett hadn't ever had the privilege of a desk job. Just this, service to the government against the water levels, since he was seventeen years old. The scar was jagged across his palm. He rubbed it thinking about that day, jumping into the water, working alongside Dan. He had made friends, saved a whale. It seemed like such a long time ago, yet mere days. He would miss those guys, that ship, that freedom. He had his head shaved and changed into his fatigues and boots, ready for his return to service.

Then he sat in a hallway outside a door while his paperwork was completed. Waiting. Wishing he had his watch. *Why the hell was it taking this long?* His three hours was ticking by.

Finally a secretary handed him his release forms paper-clipped to his service forms, and without any irony at all told Beckett he was free to go.

Beckett raced to the hallway where Sarah and Dan were waiting to drive him to see Luna.

Chapter 45

Dan circled the big lot three times before he double parked behind a tiny blue car near the back. "This car is a friend of Chickadee's, he's not going to leave anytime soon. So this is it, you ready? It's not pretty."

The sky was sagging, dark, thick, and heavy with rain. A drizzle seeped out, not raining down as much as thoroughly wetting everything as if from every direction. The windshield wipers swept back and forth with a flimp-floomp noise. Beckett said, "You're kind of freaking me out, how bad can it be?"

Sarah turned around in her seat. "We just need you to be ready for the conditions."

"The rain—what conditions?"

Dan asked, "Do we have time to look for an umbrella or ponchos? We're going to be soaked through."

Beckett said, "I'm down to an hour."

Dan said, "Okay, then. We should go. Wet never hurt anyone."

They all opened their car doors, stepped out, and were already soaked through.

Beckett followed Dan. "Do we go up to the building?"

Dan said, "You, my friend, as a relative of Chickadee's, are not welcome at the building."

"Oh. But Luna is okay, right?"

"Sure, enough."

Beckett followed Dan and Sarah through the rain — across the big sprawling completely full parking lot, to a sloping lawn that ended at a big chain-link fence.

Visibility was low in the grey gloomy rain, but Beckett made out a large group milling in front of the fence. Walking closer, he could see umbrellas, camp chairs, tents, tables and close to sixty people. As he entered the crowd behind Roscoe, Beckett recognized friends from back home.

People welcomed him, shook his hand, crowded around. People that he didn't expect — his former football coach, his former science teacher, Chickadee's film crew.

And then Chickadee.

"Beckie!!!!" She threw her arms around his neck, holding him tight to her soft jiggling front, rocking him back and forth. Dilly threw her arms around them both, creating a huddle. Beckett buried his face in their shoulders. And they told him how much they missed him, loved him, and then he looked up.

Luna.

There, on the inside of a chain-link fence.

Beckett pulled away from his Aunts's embrace. "What's happening?" He swung his head up and down and around taking in the scope of the pen. His eyes darted along the back, noticing the Waterfolk huddled under the tree line, seeking shelter from the rain. "What is this?"

Chickadee grasped both sides of his face, "Beckie these are the camps, please don't get upset, your Auntie has this all under—"

146

"What are you—" He picked up a section of the chain that connected her waist to Luna's pen.

"I've chained myself to this fence." Hoarsely, she yelled over her shoulder in the direction of a building, "And I will not leave until our Luna is out!" To the crowd she bellowed, "Is anyone going to leave until everyone gets to leave?"

The crowed around her yelled, "Hell no!"

"See Aunt Chickadee is going to get Luna out of here. Now what happened with your case?"

Beckett eyes returned to Luna over his aunt's shoulder, a few feet away, separated by a crowd and that fence, and the necessity of speaking to Chickadee and Dilly first. "I get to meet my battalion. I have to serve six months. I go in an hour." Luna's smile fell, her eyes brimmed with tears. Beckett scrubbed his hand over his newly shaved head. "Look, Chickadee, I have to speak to Luna."

"Yes, Beckie, of course you do."

She stepped aside, the crowd parted, and he strode to the fence.

Chapter 46

He hooked his hands through the fence, and planted his feet wide to lower himself, near eye to eye. "God, I'm so glad to see you. Luna, this isn't how this was supposed to..."

"I know..."

"I'm so sorry." Beckett scanned the pen. People were huddled, dripping, wet, cold. He looked back at Luna, her hair was plastered down, sopping, her clothes too thin, stuck to her shivering skin. "I'm so sorry. Were you scared?"

Luna nodded. "Really scared — about a lot of things."

"About me?" Rain dripped down his face, he wiped his face and shook his fingers spraying water away.

"Yes."

"That I was okay?"

"Yes and..."

"More?"

She chewed her lip. "That I had made a mistake. That I traveled here, across the ocean, just because you asked, that it was too much for me to do."

Beckett nodded. "Yeah, I get that. This is not—" He rattled the fence. "Not at all." Beckett leaned his forehead on the fence. "I won't be there. You heard that I have to go?"

"For six whole months?"

"Yeah, I'm so sorry. How do you stick with me after all of this? How do you trust me?"

Luna smiled sadly and joked. "I don't see how, you promised me you'd drive me and my paddleboard home on your motorcycle. I've been looking forward to watching you work through the logistics of that promise."

"I'm not sure that's exactly what I said."

Luna asked, "Do you see all these people behind me? They're Waterfolk. Just like me, like my family." She turned and pointed at a group huddled under the trees in the far end. "That family's surname is the Hymenopteras. I found out that they are actually distant cousins. One of the men was very fond of my uncle, and I don't even have to ask. I can join them. But I won't."

Beckett watched her face and asked, "Would they go back out?"

"Yes, once they're released. They'll get their boards back, and they're gone."

He blew out a gust of air. "I bet you could ask them to take you to Sky's family. I mean, you should, six whole months I'll be gone."

Luna squinted her eyes. "Are you taking away my home? You freaking promised me a home, are you taking it away?"

"No never I just wonder if you would be happier."

Luna sighed, "Beckett, I'm standing in a cage, I came all this way, what are you even talking about? See that family there, the Celastrinas, they have a son, Springer, they'd like me to travel with them, because they think he and I should be together."

He said, "Oh god."

"Yes, exactly Beckett, but I'm staying. I'm telling you this because I really need you to understand why. To not have any doubts."

Luna wrapped her fingers around his in the fence links. "The truth is that I have family and fellow Water-folk over on that side of the pen, it's familiar, and it's drier there, shadier, but this is where I'm standing. Over here by you. This is where I keep standing, talking to Chickadee, listening to my new friends. They love you so much and now they love me too, so though I've given more thought to a good hitch knot than I gave to coming to shore, I'm not scared about it anymore, about you. I'm here, and you weren't here, you won't be, but it's okay. I'm here. And I'll be waiting for you when you get home."

Tears welled up in Beckett's eyes. "Thank you."

"Do you feel better?"

"Yep, by degrees."

She shivered.

"Are you cold?"

"Yes, but a little water never hurt anyone." She gave him a sad smile.

Beckett sighed. "Dan just said something very similar. Speaking of water, I have a bus to catch, to go throw sandbags. I'll get a break though. In three months I'll get a weekend. I'll see you somewhere."

Luna said, "At your house. There's no way Chickadee lets this last three months. She'll burn it down first."

Beckett smiled. "You're in good hands."

"Definitely."

"And Roscoe is the best. He'll get everyone out, it's just a matter of time. I didn't know — you see that right? I didn't know this about the camps."

"Not one person believes you did."

Beckett blew out a breath of air. "Are we cursed?"

Luna looked at the chain-link separating them. "Some might say so, but I prefer my friend's opinion, that you and I are living an epic love story."

"Is this Chickadee we're talking about? She told me I needed to be with someone who helped me write the punchline of my life's sitcom, or something like that."

Chickadee chuckled merrily, "I'm sitting right behind you. If you're going to quote me, get it right."

Luna asked Beckett, "What would your punchline be?"

"I'm not sure — maybe it's something about how the girl I'm writing it with and I are never alone together." Beckett glanced over his shoulder at the crowd gathered around them.

"We Waterfolk are never alone, no one would find that funny. I think your punchline is that you volunteered."

Beckett smiled, "True that, or what about — man terrified of ocean finds himself inside the ocean, lots of ocean."

"You jumped."

Beckett chuckled. "That's our punchline, 'and then we jumped.' Now we have to write the joke."

"In six months."

Beckett groaned. "If I have to be away from you that long I need more to think about. I know your birthday is August 15th, and you're learning how to dance. And that you are slowly falling in love with Calvin and Hobbes and that you paddle like a badass. And you have my grandfather's — wait where's my grandfather's watch?"

"They took it when they forcibly showered me."

Chickadee struggled out of her chair with a, "Oh, hell no!"

Beckett smirked. "Chickadee you heard that?"

"I certainly did. This travesty will not be allowed to continue. That is stolen property. Roscoe! Roscoe!"

Dilly said, "Chickie dear, Roscoe left to deliver your morning filings to the court administrator."

Chickadee, rain pouring down her face, said, "Mark it someone, mark this moment, I will get my grandfather's watch back from these evil people for Luna and Beckett if it's the last thing I do!" She plopped down into the chair sending her chain rattling.

Beckett chuckled and leaned his forehead against the fence again. They looked into each other's eyes. He said, "Tell me something about you that I don't know."

Luna said, "Hmmm, a big thing?"

She stared off into space. She considered telling Beckett the really big thing, the terrible thing, about the night she lost her family, but speaking the words would hurt. They would hurt in her heart and her throat and she didn't know if she could take that much pain. And it would cause him pain too — he might — she didn't want to think about what he might think. Or say. He would feel it for all those days, what, *ninety*, until she saw him again?

So she went for simpler. "Did I tell you that it was my mother that taught me how to navigate? Usually the men do it, but my grandmother taught my mother, and she taught me. She told me to keep it secret. I loved that it was just between us.

"The way she navigated was different from the way the men navigated. My mom didn't use size and distance, she used stories and relationships. She had tales about each star and as it moved through the sky, its story would change. Story after story, she would ask me to repeat them so I would remember."

Beckett smiled. "It's like she saw the future — that you would need to find your way through the world by yourself."

"She was pretty magical."

"Can you tell me one?"

Luna brushed her thumb along the curve of his finger. "The easiest one, the first one. There's a constellation called the Monarch. It's visible in that area of the sky." Luna pointed behind Beckett.

"Southeast?"

"Yes. I believe it uses some of your constellation, Orion, the rest of it looks like a big butterfly. It's supposed to travel the skies carrying messages from one person to a far away other person. I sent you messages after I left you on the Outpost."

"I got them. One hundred percent. That's why I came to find you."

Luna screwed up her face. "I don't think the timeline—"

"Don't over-think it, the story is so much better that way. So you'll be sending me messages by the Monarch constellation every night."

"Yes, but that's not the story, not really. This, the Monarch, has moved ever so slightly north, just barely. The tip of the left wing is almost touching the Breeze constellation." She pointed up to the south. "Right there, stretching across the sky with twists, like a wind. Next time I'm with you, in three months, I'll show it to you, but until then you should try to figure it out, okay?"

"That's all I'll do."

Luna smiled.

Beckett said, "Just a minute." He pulled his hands from the fence and shook them out. "My hands hurt." He put his fingers back immediately.

Luna kissed his right hand's finger tip, and continued, "Because the Monarch's wing is in the Breeze constellation it means big changes. Disruptions and upsets, but not necessarily in the bad way. It's up to us to whisper to the Monarch what we want to happen. Begin the flow. It will be over a year that the two constellations are touching. So that's good. We have time to get the change right."

"I love you Luna."

"I love you too. Now you tell me something about your—"

Chapter 47

Dan came to the fence, "Beckett, Luna, I'm sorry to interrupt, but if I'm going to get you to the bus station in time, we should probably move."

Beckett said, "Aargh." He ran his hands over his head. "Can I run away again?"

Dan smirked, "Proving that dumbasses go army. We got your girl, none of us are leaving until she goes home. *With* your aunt Chickadee. We're out in the rain. You can trust us."

Beckett nodded, his eyes on Luna. "You'll be okay Luna, right?"

"I trust you, thcm, I'll be okay."

Chickadee stood from her chair. "Hug your Aunty, Beckie." He wrapped up in Chickadee's smothering hug. Into his ear she said, "You take care of yourself. You're doing good work, important work. You're placing sandbags keeping the water at bay. You're a hero. You go be a hero and we'll handle this. No worries."

Beckett nodded into her shoulder.

Next Dilly hugged him then she leaned back to look up at his face. "You have to keep your heart focused on the long goal, but your brain concentrating on the present time. Do what you have to do minute by minute and the moments will slide by. You'll have a weekend with us in three months. And you'll call every week. We'll be waiting."

Beckett was unable to speak he was so overcome. He was home, but he spent the whole time in jail, all that precious time — what he wouldn't do to have it back. He turned back to Luna. "I'll see you soon."

"Of course you will, and you know where to find me." She gave him a bittersweet grin.

"I do, it's a house on a mountain, northeast of here by about two hours." He gave her a sad smile. "I'm sorry I didn't tell you something to think about while I'm gone."

She said, "It's okay, I have enough."

Dan gave him another reminding pat on the shoulder and Beckett turned to go, but suddenly Luna's hand went to her stomach with a low moan.

Beckett spun. "You okay?"

She nodded, grimaced, and swallowed. "I just — ugh."

She leaned over, hands on her knees, retching. "Ugh," she said again.

Beckett crouched and peered up into her face. "Luna?"

She spit onto the cement. "Ugh, it's okay, I'm fine I —" She vomited all over her feet.

"Luna, you okay? Dr Mags!"

Dr Mags rushed the fence. "Sit down so you don't fall down."

Luna slumped to the ground. Waterfolk gathered around her. Dr Mags said, "Jeffrey go to the building. Tell them I need access to Luna." Jeffrey darted away.

Dan said, "I'm sorry to say this Beckett, but you have to go. Or you'll be late."

"I'm not going, I won't."

Dan stepped in front of Beckett. "You won't go?"

"You heard me—"

Dan stepped into Beckett's space, "What, the dumbass won't go?"

"Fuck you."

Beckett tried to step around him, but Dan planted two hands on his chest and shoved him backwards up the hill. "You going back to the fence? Because only dumbasses go back to the fence."

Beckett tried to swipe Dan's hands away.

Dan shoved him so hard that he stumbled three steps. "Dumbasses stay here."

"Stop calling me a dumbass. I'm starting to get pissed off."

"Oh yeah? Well I'm pissed off too. Look at you — with your scarred hands, your busted face, your girlfriend in a pen. And the only reason you're not in jail is because you have the best lawyer in the world, and he got you off. Well guess what — he can't do it again. You blow this chance and you'll rot in that jail or worse, East, the front. Is that what you want?" He shoved Beckett so hard he fell on the slick grassy slope.

Beckett, from down in the mud, asked, "Dan would you leave if it was Sarah? Would you leave?"

"I wouldn't want to, but I hope I'd have a friend who would kick my ass to make me. Because you friend, have to get on that bus. And if you don't leave now, you're going to miss it."

Luna raised her head and called across the crowd to Beckett, "Go, I'm fine. I didn't eat very well —" She retched and heaved again.

"I can't leave, crap, I can't—"

Dan said, "You have to. We'll give you updates — you have to go or they won't allow you to come back."

Luna wiped her mouth on her wrist. "Beckett, I have a stomach bug or something. I probably ate too many apples or. . ." She swallowed, fighting down another upheave.

Chickadee leaned into Beckett's field of vision. "What are you going to do here? Watch Luna throw up what she ate, then sit in jail? You can't help, so go. You're the first to hear when she's all better."

Luna threw up again.

Dilly said quietly, "You have to Beckett." She offered him her hand, helped him up, and turned him away toward the parking lot. Dan pulled beside him as escort.

Beckett asked, "You'll call me, right? Dan? Dilly? You'll call?"

Dan and Dilly both nodded and assured Beckett all the way to the car.

Chapter 48

The gate was opened and Dr Mags dropped to the ground beside Luna. She placed her fingers on Luna's wrist and counted. Then she asked the gathered Water-folk to load Luna onto a blanket and carry her over to the far end of the pen where it was dry.

Luna begged, "I can walk, let me walk." But Dr Mags continued counting, commanding, and hovering like Luna's stomach bug was a full blown emergency.

Once Luna landed in a spot under a tree with a large crowd gathered around, Dr Mags checked her eyes. "How long have you been feeling like this?"

"It started yesterday. It comes on like a wave."

Dr Mags asked, "What did you eat this morning and when?"

"A protein pouch and an apple. Water. About two hours ago."

"Hungry?"

"Not really. . ."

"What would taste good to you right now?"

"Chocolate, something sweet."

Dr Mags furrowed her brow. "Okay, stupid question, I'm not sure if Nomads even get government-mandated birth control, but if you do, have you been taking it?"

Luna said, "We don't. . ."

"When was your last period?"

Luna's face twisted up, "Um. I — uh. Oh."

Chapter 49

Dan searched his pockets for the keys while Beckett stared across the parking lot down the sloping grass to the faraway gathering at the fence. They were moving Luna in a blanket. He could run back there, but he shouldn't. He shouldn't do anything but leave. His only option. Beckett didn't like having only one option. Not when it came to Luna.

This sucked. If he had known that last night on the ship, when he held her under his shirt, hiding from the storm, would be the last night — if he had only known. He might have held tighter. Hell, he'd still be there.

So why was he here, back on land? Was this the whole goal — to get her here? She was in a cage and he was driving away.

Dan unlocked the car. Beckett climbed in. The engine rumbled to life.

Dan said, "I know you want to go back, but here's the thing, that's real trouble for you and also, what if they arrest you at the protest? They could say all the protesters are criminals and public opinion would turn. Right now your Aunt Chickadee, who is awesome by the way, and her friends, are fun and friendly and smart. People are watching the news and thinking they make sense. But if you show up and get all tragic and argumentative and belligerent and arrested, guess what happens?"

"They look like troublemakers."

Dan pulled the car out of the parking lot. "Opinion is changing. No one wants the trouble of dealing with this; it takes too much effort. Aunt Chickadee is making people focus on that effort and question whether it's worth it."

"You make sense — but it's still — man." Beckett ran his hands up and down on his face.

"I don't blame you. If Sarah was — I don't blame you. But at least you have Chickadee." They sped along the coastal highway toward the bus station.

Beckett stared out the window at the shops and houses flying by. "And Roscoe."

"That guy is a genius. He told me that the government spends thousands of dollars a *day* on the Nomad camps. Instead they could have expanded the Outpost system with floating derricks. It would have been a fraction of the money, but a couple of politicians, specifically John Smithsonian and his buddy at the Final Interior, Tuck Frank, thought it would be worth it. They're on some kind of evangelical mission to change the Nomads, turn them into land dwellers. Can you believe it?"

Beckett shook his head. "I was a part of it. All those people, I sent a lot of them to the camps."

"Yeah well, you didn't have the full story. We all have the full story now. And if it wasn't for you, they wouldn't have Chickadee chained to their fence."

"Chickadee is a formidable woman, you should have seen her when I. . ." Beckett's voice trailed away. He added, "I'm glad she's always been on my side."

Dan pulled into a space in front of the bus station, got out, and pulled Beckett's bag from the trunk.

Beckett said, "Promise me, if something is wrong, any news, a sneeze, God, or a cough, anything — promise me you'll let me know."

"Definitely man, I promise. I'll make sure."

"Okay, thanks." The two hugged, said goodbye, and Beckett walked slowly toward the bus station.

Dan yelled, "Shoulders straight Army. You need a strong back for all that sandbag lifting!"

Beckett raised his hand with a wave and disappeared into the cavernous building.

Chapter 50

Luna heaved herself into a sitting position with a groan. She rested her head on her knees for a moment, then said, "I'm okay now. I can walk. I should go tell Chickadee I'm okay."

Dr Mags walked with Luna through the sprinkling rain toward Chickadee's encampment, where a guard gestured for the doctor to leave the cage. He slammed the door closed with a clank, almost in Luna's face, and locked it with added animosity.

Chickadee glared at him. "You mark my words, I will have your job." Then she turned with a sweet smile to the fence and Luna behind it. "Are you okay, Dear?"

Luna nodded.

Dr Mags said, "Can Luna and I speak to you alone?"

Chickadee turned flapping her arms. "Shoo, shoo." The surrounding crowd got up and shifted away.

Luna said, "I need to sit down." She collapsed into a cross legged position.

Chickadee clutched the fence. "I'm sorry, but you still don't look good dear. I think you need a hospital. Don't worry I'll get you to—"

Dr Mags said, "Chickadee, I believe Luna might be pregnant."

"Pregnant?"

Luna nodded.

"With Beckie's baby?"

Luna nodded again.

"Oh, *honey*." Chickadee's eyes swept around the pen and the surrounding encampment, it was all sadly, terribly, bleak. "Oh honey. Now this is amazing news but. . . You're inside a—" She turned to Dr Mags. "Will the baby make it? I mean, it's so rare. . ."

Dr Mags shrugged. "It's rare to even get pregnant, who knows. We'll need to run a lot of tests. I have a friend at the Heighton Hospital that Luna can see."

Chickadee ran her hands up and down her face. "What is Beckett going to — he'll come back here. He'll get himself arrested."

Dan appeared through the crowd, arm thrown around Sarah, headed their way. When they were close enough, Dan grinned. "Man, Army barely got on the bus. I had to watch the doors to make sure he didn't desert again. And I hope Luna is okay now, because I promised I'd report back, pronto." His expression dropped. "What?"

Dr Mags and Chickadee looked from Dan and Sarah to Luna. She bit her lip and screwed up her face. "I'm probably pregnant."

Dan's eyes opened wide. "Oh. *Oh*. Oh man."

Sarah slapped her hand over her mouth. "Oh!" She crouched down eye level with Luna. "Luna what will you do?"

"I need to talk to Beckett—"

Dan said, "Definitely. He needs to know."

Luna nodded and sat for a while staring off into space. Then she turned to Dr Mags. "What are the odds?"

"I have limited knowledge, but carrying a baby to term is increasingly rare. Is it rare for Waterfolk too?"

"It's rare to have babies, but also complicated. I'm not sure many Waterfolk families want to. It means they have to split up, live on land for a bit, drastically change their circumstances. We usually try not to, and I just, I don't — I guess I forgot that I would—"

Chickadee said, "You would what, dear?"

Luna twisted the hem of her cotton dress. "I forgot that I would keep living."

Chickadee said, "Well, you did dear, and we are so grateful for that. But now we need to call Beckett, immediately."

Dan said, "Yes, he's waiting, worried already. I *promised*. But he'll come back here for sure if you tell him."

Luna nodded. "I don't — wait, let me think." Luna sat for a moment. She dug her fingers into the mud and thought about what this meant, to her, Luna, Waterfolk. Pregnancy meant that you had to look for a nesting spot. A place to rest. A place to have the baby. A place to nurse the baby until you could move again. And wasn't that what her plan already was, nesting?

It was a good plan.

Beckett, without even knowing, was giving her a nest.

She only had to get there.

And she had to get him there.

Safely.

And she had no idea if the baby would make it. So many didn't, so she had to go with the flow.

She was good at that. It was in her DNA. Trouble was she was surrounded by stiff-neck, land-dwellers who would want to stop everything and fix it. She looked up in their faces, they were worried and afraid.

She would need to make sure she stayed strong. And kept Beckett safe. That was the only thing to do.

She took a deep long breath, stood, and swiped the gravel off the back of her legs. "We won't tell Beckett. Not yet. Not until he comes back in three months."

Sarah, crouched beside her in the rain, asked, "Are you sure?"

Chickadee said "It seems like something he ought to know, even if it—"

Luna said, "You said so yourself, he'll come back. He'll get himself arrested. I need him. I have to keep him safe. I owe him that. Even if it means keeping this from him. That's my decision. No one can tell Beckett."

Dan said, "I think he deserves the right to hear about this, but also, so far, he has terrible decision-making skills. And worse where Luna is concerned. So, I guess I agree with Luna. For what it's worth. New friend and all."

Sarah nodded. "New friend vote, I agree with Dan and Luna — yes. And oh Luna, I'm so—a baby, really?"

Dan reached down and squeezed her hand.

Chickadee squinted her eyes. "Fine, I'm in agreement. We won't tell him until he comes home in three months."

They nodded at each other solemnly.

Until Dan said, "But seriously, what am I going to tell Army?"

"Tell him I'm fine, it was something I ate."

Chapter 51

"Hey Dan, what's the news?"

Dan stood in the middle of the parking lot, staring back at the camps. "By the time I got back, Luna felt totally better."

"Really? What did Dr Mags say?"

"She said it was something Luna ate, acted like I was an asshole for worrying about it. You know Dr Mags, all business when you're sick, but when you're healthy, she's the first to tell you to suck it up. Well she told me to tell you that Luna said to suck it up. She's fine."

"Man, that is such a relief."

"Are you with your battalion yet?"

"Still on the bus, though we're entering the mountains, I might lose service soon. I have two hours left."

"Why are you going into the mountains? Aren't you headed to the coast? I thought—"

Beckett ran his hand around his head. "Can you put Luna on the phone? Hold it for her through the fence?"

Dan looked around the parking lot, "Um, I'm not with her right now. I stepped away to make this call, sorry man. I'll do it in a bit."

Beckett closed his eyes. "I'm not sure if I can talk much after six, try to call before, okay?"

"Look, it's no problem I'm walking back right now." Dan jogged across the parking lot toward the fence, reaching it, and looking at the phone. Beckett wasn't there.

"Luna, I'm sorry Beckett wanted to talk to you." He dialed Beckett's number. The call was answered by a strange beep-beep sound. "Weird. I guess we lost the connection. He said he was going into the mountains. . ."

Chickadee said, "The mountains? There's no mountains near the coast where he'll be stationed. . ." Her voice trailed off.

Dan nodded with a glance at Luna. "You know, I probably misheard him. we'll call back in a few minutes, see if we can't get him on the phone again."

Chapter 52

The following day Beckett called Chickadee.

"Beckie!!!" She yelled into the phone, then to everyone else, "Beckie's on the phone!!"

"Hi Chickadee, are you still with Luna at the camps?"

"Oh we are, we're all here, and the crowd is even bigger now. Hey everyone say, 'Hi Beckie!'"

A cacophony of voices yelled his name. She said, "Roscoe has the hearing set for Thursday, three days from now. He said this was merely a formality."

"That's amazing Chickadee, this is quite an accomplishment."

"All I did was plant myself like a brick wall. It's pretty much all I'm suited for. Don't tell Dilly I said that, she'll get all romantic and make me sit still and listen to her list off my assets in long form poetry, but really she has to say that because she loves me. Those that don't love me know — I'm stubborn as a brick wall. It's what they say behind my back. I'm a realist."

"I agree with Dilly, you're amazing."

"You should save your long form poetry for Luna." She giggled. "She wants to speak to you, I'll hold the phone to the fence, so don't say anything lewd, because I'll probably hear it." She grunted as she rose from the chair.

Beckett said, "Lewd? You're the one talking about my long form poetry."

She cackled merrily. "It's not really you I'm worried about, it's Luna who would, wouldn't you dear?"

Luna gave her a weak smile, took a deep gulp of edifying air, and sat up from her sprawled position on a blanket on the ground. Her nausea had been terrible all day, but she wanted to talk to Beckett more than anything. Her next few moments would be very difficult to maneuver.

"Hi!" She forced herself to sound upbeat.

"Hey love, last I saw you you were spewing chunks all over your feet." He laughed. "Dan says you're good?"

"Yeah, I'm great. And it stopped raining, so — everything is good here."

"I'm so glad. I miss you so much."

"I miss you too, though I'm getting used to it,"

Beckett sat for a moment. "You're getting used to it?"

"Yes, I mean, we've been apart so much it's just normal. I didn't mean I didn't miss you, I—"

"Yeah, no, I get it. We've been apart a lot."

"Beckett, I just meant that I'm okay, that this is going to be okay, us being apart."

Beckett ran his hand over his head. "Wait, I need to hang up, my commanding officer wants me."

"Okay, I love you, I miss you, I really do, I just wanted you to know that I was okay—" Luna looked down at the phone — the call was lost. She burst into tears. "I said it all wrong, and he — this is too hard."

Chickadee said, "I know dearest, you're going to have a lot of difficult conversations for the next little while. It will be hard, but he knows. Don't worry yourself, he'll understand."

Chapter 53

Beckett's phone rang three days later — Chickadee. "We won! that Roscoe is a genius and we won, and all the—"

The sound of celebrating drowned out her next words. Beckett said, "That's awesome Chickadee! I'm so—"

She continued, "Roscoe was so eloquent, brilliant. Those bureaucrats didn't even know how to begin to argue against him. They asked at most ten questions, deliberated for an hour and then said they would close the camps." More cheering from the surrounding voices.

Beckett said, "So is Luna there?"

"Roscoe is so amazing. Here, Dilly wants to talk to you!"

Dilly came to the phone. "Your Aunt Chickadee really did it this time."

"That she did."

"It looks like the camp closure will be in effect by the end of the month—" She yelled, "Woohooo!" to someone off the phone, then returned her attention to Beckett. "So we have lots of celebrating to do."

"I'm so glad, is Luna there?"

"Hey, it's really loud in here. I love you, and we're so proud of you. I hope your back doesn't hurt too much from all that sandbag lifting. I'm giving you back to Chickadee."

Beckett shut his eyes tight as Chickadee came back on the phone. "I knew you wanted to be the first to hear. Your Luna will be home soon."

"When will she get to go home?"

"What did you say? When you'll come home? I can't hear you over the party, I'll call tomorrow and—"

"Sure, of course, but tomorrow, after that it will be harder to get through."

"Okay, bye Beckie!!"

Chapter 54

The following day Beckett received a call from Chickadee's phone, but Luna's voice greeted him. "I'm out."

Relief surged through his body. "Oh I'm so glad Luna, I'm so glad. I don't — I'm speechless."

"Me too. I'm so happy and grateful and excited and kind of scared. We're in the truck. Dilly and Chickadee are driving me to your mountain house. Or less driving, more sitting and waiting, traffic is terrible."

Beckett leaned against the wall. "Tell me where you are. . ."

She conversed off phone for a moment. "We're nearing the blackened bridge. Dilly said to tell you that the troll still lives under it."

"Tell Dilly I haven't ever believed her."

Luna said, "She stuck out her tongue."

"Tell Dilly she's acting like a five-year-old." He sighed. "I wish I could be there with you."

"Me too, but you are. I feel you all around me. And I love you so much."

"Did you get your paddleboard back?"

"I did. It's strapped in the bed of the truck right now. And our clothes from the ship. Dan and Sarah and Rebecca and Dr Mags, they all say hi by the way, and Dan said for you to do like he does and always check your surroundings in case you spring a leak."

Beckett chuckled, less because it was funny, more because he was supposed to find it funny.

After all those years of thinking the water was the worst thing he could think of he had finally found something worse. Far worse.

And he had talked to himself beforehand, he was supposed to not let Luna know, to not let on what was happening. He didn't want to worry her.

He asked, "And the camps will be closed by next month?"

"Most of the Waterfolk are leaving, but some are staying. There's actually some settlements opening for them, if they want to remain on land. But most of them want to head out on the high seas again."

Beckett nodded, regretting every moment of edict reading he ever did. Going east never did anyone any good. What was East? Land and more land and what did anyone do with land anymore? Fight over its dwindling size — no, he wouldn't advise anyone to head east.

Beckett coughed.

Luna asked, "Are you okay?"

"I'm okay. It's just air quality. Luna I—"

"Yes?"

"I won't be able to talk for a while. I've been in a training camp, and I leave tomorrow. I was told there wouldn't be phone service, a lot like being on the Outpost."

Luna said, "Oh." She watched the trees glide by outside her window as traffic inched forward. "For how long?"

"Maybe months."

Tears welled in Luna's eyes. "What about coming home in three months?"

He said, "Thank you for calling it home. That means a lot to me."

"But will you, come home in three months?"

"I don't know. It might not be possible."

"Oh."

Beckett's chest squeezed so tight he thought he might not be able to breathe. "I love you. I want you to know I'm thinking about you when I'm not there. Every minute."

"Me too. Plus, the Monarch constellation."

"Yeah. Look Luna, I have to go. I'm being called to dinner."

"But it's early afternoon."

"Oh yeah, um, but it's time for me to go."

"But you're in the same time zone, aren't you, Beckett? Just down the coast?"

Chickadee said, "Tell him we can drive down there, we can come for the weekend, anytime."

Luna said, "If you can't come home we can come see you on the base. Whenever you have a day off. . ."

"I think our connection is bad again, I'll call when I get a—" He hung up the phone and tossed it in his lap.

Crap. Six months. This was too much. He tried to think about Luna walking up the front steps of his home, Luna sleeping curled up in his bed, Luna smiling in his living room waiting for him to come home after a long day — but it all seemed imaginary, fake, like a photograph of a perfect life before all this bullshit.

He picked up his helmet and put it on his head. Grabbed his gun and surveyed the scene — this was one bleak shit storm of a disaster.

Chapter 55

Smoke filled air, rubbled buildings, pillaged towns, buildings that were wrecked bombed and ransacked. He was supposed to protect this. Not with sandbags, but with his life now. Because the thing was, until the next big leveling, it was all water coming up, nothing you could do but scrabble higher. And guess what? Everyone wanted higher land.

And here in the East, around the industry and power and energy, the factories full of making shit to do shit with, this place, it was what everyone wanted. Because the last one standing with a factory, they win.

And here was Beckett, last six months of his six year tour, and his job was to make sure that he was one of the last men. Or die trying.

He could have told her of course that there had been a change of orders. That his battalion wasn't doing sandbags anymore. They were doing this — fighting over the scraps that were left.

But really what was the point — It was like he was gone already. Heavy heart, smoky lungs, shit to conquer. Nah, better to keep this to himself. Tell her after the fact. If he survived. . .

Chapter 56

"But you said you could, we have plans…" Luna was sitting in a rocking chair on the front porch of Beckett's mountain house. The sun was setting, lighting the sky in a pink glow.

"I know, I wish it could be different. I just can't come. They won't let me, there's so much going on here — they've cut off all vacation for a month and sadly my weekend falls in the middle of it." Beckett shook in the vibrating rumble of a far-off explosion.

"What's that noise?"

"A train probably. Seriously, I miss you so much, if I could, if they let me have the time, I would be there in a second."

"When do you think you can come home?" Behind Luna, through the screen door in the kitchen, Dilly was cooking dinner. By now Luna had grown used to the comforting sounds — pots lightly clanging, water splashing, jars, cans opening, spilling, shaking, and through it all, Chickadee at the kitchen counter, working on some project, a screenplay, or really anything she had thought up that week, talking about her work. Dilly would say, "Uh huh," when her thoughts were on the food, and occasionally, "Exactly!" when her thoughts were on Chickadee's project. Because Dilly agreed with Chickadee on most everything, being, in Luna's estimation, one of the most agreeable people in the world.

Chickadee was strong-willed, and bossy, kind, but also certain and stubborn, prone to big ideas and constant implementation. Dilly on the other hand was empathetic and loving, nurturing and sweet. She had a poem for every situation.

Luna loved them both, but she especially loved talking to Dilly, because Dilly woke up in the night and sat with Luna on the porch, for hours, if that's what it took to calm Luna's mind.

Dilly got the In-Betweens as Luna's mother used to say. The stuff inside the pauses between the words. The down deep.

Beckett's voice brought her back to their conversation. "Since I'm missing the three month visit, they'll definitely grant me the next leave. Once they lift the moratorium. I've put my name in, as soon as they tell me, I'll call . . ."

"Oh, okay."

Luna wished she was better at the In-Betweens. She was better when she was out on the ocean, but here on a porch, in a strange place, on a phone, she was out of her element. She was sure Beckett wasn't telling her everything, but without knowing enough about how this world worked, she couldn't guess.

"Could I come?" She pulled her knees up and rested her head there. "Chickadee said she would drive me, even if it's just for a few hours."

"They won't let us have visitors, it might get me in trouble."

"That's what Dilly thought too. I was really hoping to talk to you about some—" Her hand rested on her small rounded stomach.

"What? Are you okay — is something going on?"

She clenched her eyes shut. "No, I'm good. It's nothing. I just miss you so much."

"I miss you too. And it's only going to be a week or two, three at the most, and they'll grant my leave and — we've only got two-and-a-half months left. We're over halfway there."

"Yes, sure, time will fly."

"And you'll be there? I mean, I know, but I — you will right? You're happy living there?"

"Yes, I'm happy. I'm also heartbroken." A tear slid down her cheek. "Neither of those things will make me leave."

"I'm glad. Knowing you're there is the only thing that keeps me going. I'll call you next week."

Chapter 57

Luna found Dilly walking along the edge of the corn rows, near the lavender walkway, spiraling around talking to herself, the way she always did when she was writing a poem. "Can I interrupt?"

"Of course Luna, I'm singing to the bees, a little ditty masquerading itself as a poem, but you'll hear tomorrow night at our gathering." Dilly was wearing overalls, a tube top stretched across her chest. Her hair was, as she often said, "Growing out because it had lost all reason." It was going gray, and Dilly, perturbed, had decided to wear it long in protest. Flowers stuck out of her hair in a few places, and the ends of her hair stuck out in all directions, curly. She called it "insensible" and "ornery."

"I was hoping to talk to you, I wanted to see how you were faring after your conversation last night with Beckett?"

Luna dropped into a garden chair. "I'm okay — or, not, but . . ." Luna stared over the hedgerow. Bees spun up and around in a busy circle. Watching bees was a new experience for Luna. Her circular thoughts used to follow eddies, and currents, not insects, but here she was on a mountainside among the bees. "I don't know what to think, I feel like Beckett isn't telling me something."

Dilly nodded slowly. "I agree. He has a big thing, something he sees, that he can't tell you about. And you have a big thing, something you feel, that you can't tell him about. And the things, big things, are piling around you both."

"I want to tell him. I was planning to tell him today. Here."

"Yet his big thing, is keeping him from learning your big thing. And so it goes. I sense it too, and I wish I could advise you better. But this — Beckett loves you. He must feel like what he's seeing, or doing, is too big to tell you about. He might be wrong. I have known you now for a little over three months, not long, not long enough to know your story, just little things, the way you circle the house in the night, the way you cry curled up when you can't sleep, the way you stare off into the horizon at dusk, the way you look at the stars, and even the way you laugh, truly letting go with joy, a joy like that means there's a sadness there too — you can't have one without the other. But all those things makes me believe Beckett is wrong — you're strong enough to hear what he believes he needs to hide." Dilly dropped into a garden chair beside Luna.

"I am. I can handle it. Should I tell him I can?"

"Maybe. But sometimes something is so scary it's hard to be fearless enough to even tell someone about it. You might need to accept that he's hiding something, but he doesn't want to, but he has to. You might have to trust him even so."

"Oh. I never thought about that."

"You have things too. Beyond the baby. Things you're not fearless enough to tell. Right?" Dilly peered into Luna's face.

Luna nodded.

"It's the words. They can be really hard. Sometimes it can be nice if the person you love hears you without speaking a word."

Luna's eyes drifted up to the sky. "So I shouldn't pack my suitcase and drive to his base and demand he tells me what he's hiding?"

Dilly squinted her eyes. "You know as well as I do that he's not there."

Luna nodded. "Yeah, he's in the east, fighting."

Dilly followed Luna's eyes to the sky. "This was not what Beckett was supposed to be doing. Chickadee and I have devoted the last fifteen years to keeping him safe. But here he is. All we can do is sing to the bees begging them for distraction like me, or like Chickadee does, write congressmen, or like you—?"

"I whisper to him by the Monarch Constellation."

Dilly squeezed Luna's hand. "And that is a perfectly poetical thing to say. It's all we can do, this — and wait."

"And hope it's enough."

"The rest is up to Beckett coming home."

Chapter 58

Luna entered the kitchen, just showered and dressed for the night. "How do I look?"

Dilly was kneading the last fluff of dough for the party and her arms from the elbow down were coated in flour. "Beautiful, like the gossamer wings of a dragonfly."

Chickadee looked up from her notebook. "Bullshit, you're insulting dear Luna's family heritage. She looks beautiful like the soft wings of a moth."

"You're both correct. But more to the point — do I look pregnant? I don't want to look pregnant, not until Beckett knows." She pulled the cardigan open and turned back and forth, showing off her protruding stomach.

Dilly cocked her head to the left and right. "The cardigan covers it, perfectly."

Chickadee added, "Perfectly as if you've swallowed a watermelon half-down —

Dilly said, "Chickie!"

"It's true!"

Luna giggled. "It's totally true." Then her mood spiraled downward. "I thought I would have more time, but when Beckett comes home, I'll have to hide behind a chair until I tell him."

Chickadee came around the counter and tugged Luna's cardigan closed. "He'll come home. You'll tell him.

Then you get to start your lives, both of you in the same place. No worries, right? We have poetry to read!"

Luna nodded, sniffling to cover the tears that threatened to come.

Chickadee returned her are of the counter that was her designated office. "I plan to read a Shakespearean sonnet, it is beautiful and has been revered for centuries, and I will read it directly to Dilly and everyone will ooh and aah, until she stands up. She'll read a, Little Ditty, as she will call it, that she wrote herself, about wild grass—"

"Bees," said Dilly, rolling a pin across her flattened dough.

"Bees — and she will turn a phrase, coat a word, and spin a phrase until we are all weeping with joy and laughing with sadness, and everyone will forget my dumbass Shakespearean poem."

Dilly grabbed Chickadee's face and gave her a kiss leaving a powdery handprint on her cheek. "Thanks babe, that's why I write poetry, for the glory."

Chickadee wiped her cheek with a towel. "That's how it goes, Luna, try to read your poem before her poem. That's all I'm saying."

"I was going to recite a poem my mother told me about dolphins."

Dilly clapped her hands, sending up a cloud of dust. "Perfect! Let me toss this dough in the oven and we'll get the chairs set up in the garden."

Chapter 59

A couple of hours later, Dan, Sarah, and Rebecca, arrived through the gate and Luna bounded across the lawn.

Dan merrily called, "Where's Beckett?"

"He's not coming, he couldn't—" Sarah and Rebecca swept Luna into a hug.

Dan said, "Not coming? Oh no, I came to talk to him about the—"

Sarah nudged his ribs. "Shush, keep it quiet, don't tell the whole neighborhood."

Dan deposited the cheese and cracker tray he brought for the potluck, to the appetizer table. "Yeah, you're right, it's just every day that goes by I feel like he's going to be more pissed."

Luna nodded. "It might be weeks before he can come home. And now his phone doesn't seem to be working."

"Oh Luna, I'm so sorry!" Sarah hugged her again.

People began to arrive. First, an older couple. Then a group of young women not much older than Luna. Another group of ten wandered in from the other direction. Then more people came — some from the action at the camps, a few from a dinner party weeks ago, many from the Wednesday farmer's market, and a couple from the gas station.

Chairs were set out in rows in front of a raised platform that acted as the impromptu stage. Luna, Dan, Sarah and Rebecca filled their plates and found seats in the front row. The crickets were singing, the sky was darkening, the little strings of lights were twinkling, and Luna thought it was the most beautiful, festive, wonderful night, except Beckett wasn't there, of course, but almost perfect.

And then a minute later a young woman sat beside Luna.

With a glance, Luna immediately recognized her. She was the girl from the photos on Beckett's dresser. One of them was of Beckett kissing this girl's cheek. The photos were in frames, the portraits full of smiles and hugs — they were gone now, Dilly had hustled them into a drawer out of the way, but Luna could open the drawer easily enough and study them if she wanted to. She didn't want to, but she did look sometimes, anyway.

The young woman from the photo turned to Luna. "I'm Dryden Jones, Beckett's friend. And you are?"

Luna's hands instinctively checked to make sure her cardigan was closed. "Luna."

"Luna? Beckett's never mentioned a Luna. Are you from around here?"

Luna said, "Um, I'm not, I'm—"

Rebecca nudged Sarah, who leaned forward. "Luna and I met Beckett at sea, when he was on the Outpost."

Dryden shifted in her seat and searched the crowd. "I haven't seen him yet . . ."

"He's not coming," Luna said. "He didn't get his leave."

"And how on earth do you know that? He didn't mention it to me." Dryden laughed loudly. "He'll probably just show up. That would be so Beckett, wouldn't it?" She flipped her hair, turned to her friends, and spoke loudly enough for Luna to hear. "I heard Beckett's aunts had gone all in helping the Nomads, but I didn't realize they were being allowed to set up camps here at the farm."

Red climbed up Luna's ears.

Rebecca said under her breath, "It's okay, Luna, don't let her bother you."

Sarah reached across and patted Luna on the hand, but it was all too much, even the pity, too much.

Luna's plight hit her like a slap across the face. Maybe she was a guest who had over-stayed her welcome. Maybe Beckett hadn't really meant forever. Maybe he meant, come live with me, and we'll see how it goes. Wasn't that exactly what he said?

And he left and — and — he didn't even call, barely ever.

Was he calling this other girl? Was she his mountain girl, the one that broke his heart, that he had been pining for when Luna interrupted him on the Outpost?

Luna glanced at Dryden's face. She was pale with light brown cascading hair. Her cheekbones were strong. And Luna had trouble with this one most: she was tall.

Waterfolk didn't want to be tall, but here on land, tall was best, more attractive, better. Hell, she had chosen Beckett, one of the tallest people she had ever met.

She had chosen Beckett, but had Beckett chosen her?

Luna was hiding Beckett's baby, living in his home, keeping a secret, ingratiating herself to his Aunts, acting as if she was part of his family. She had even used his last name.

She couldn't stand up there and recite a poem in front of these people. She was a stranger in their midst. They were Beckett's friends, and he wasn't there to introduce her.

Plus, and this was a big, big, big plus, her hormones were raging. She was crying constantly. The other night she had been watching one of Chickadee's favorite shows, a comedy, and had laughed until she cried, peeing her pants a little, and then cried some more because she was such a wreck.

Beckett's aunts had been so nice about it.

But seriously, she couldn't stand up there, a big wreck of a secret-keeping, overly emotional, possible-usurper of someone else's man. She couldn't do it.

Chickadee took the stage. Her hair was up in a spiky Aquamarine Mohawk. She was wearing a t-shirt that said, "Aloha!" And vibrant flowers were printed all over her tent-like skirt. She spoke into the microphone, "Hello Charlesville Adjacent Unincorporated Farm community! Welcome to Dilly's willy-hilly poetry slam. As you know, this here world is getting wetter, the sun is getting hotter, the news more terrifying, the refugees, oy, but hey, when things get bad like this, it's time to read poetry. Aren't I right Dillybear?"

Dilly said, "Right you are."

Chickadee grinned down at her. "Of course I'm right, in everything. I picked you, and that was the rightest of them all." She looked out at the audience. "First, I'm going to read a poem I want to dedicate to Dilly, the love of my life, the most beautiful woman I ever saw . . ."

Luna felt a big cry coming. She dropped her plate on the grass by her feet and raced for house.

A few seconds behind Dilly rushed in. She didn't say anything but, "Oh sweetie," and folded Luna up in a hug. "I should have seen her sit beside you, but my focus was elsewhere."

Luna sobbed into her shoulder.

"I know. I know," Dilly said, in her way, knowing, without needing to be told. Finally, after a few moments, Dilly took Luna's face in her hands, and wiped tears from her cheeks. "Beckett loves you. He told me so. And he meant it. And he is a man of his word. And Chickie and I love you, and you live here now, this is your home."

Chickadee rushed in the house, banging the screen door in her hurry. "What happened — did that girl say something to you?"

"Not really," Luna sniveled. "She made it sound as if Beckett has been calling her."

"There's no way."

"But how do you know?" Luna's lower lip trembled.

"Because after Beckett dated her, after she broke his heart, after he was sad about it for a short while, he told me he was glad to be done with her because, and this is a direct quote, 'she was the least interesting, most boring person in the world.' That's why."

Luna giggled and sobbed at the same time.

Chickadee clucked, put her hands on her hips. "Poor, poor, sweet Luna, your tears are staining your beautiful party face. Now I think you need to sit here in your rocking chair, swish back and forth, stare out over the lawn party, and cry over your Beckett. But, and I'm sorry to say this, you can't. Not while Dryden is here. I can't allow you to cede Dilly's poetry slam to that girl and her yammering friends. You must come to the front row, hold Dilly's hand, eat chocolate-covered strawberries, and applaud all the lame poetry."

Dilly said, "I agree with Chickadee, you can't hide away, you're too bad ass for that. You should read your poem and—"

Luna shook her head, her eyes wide. "I can't stand up in front of everyone, not until Beckett is here, it just feels . . ."

Dilly appraised her for a moment. "Okay, but you must applaud the loudest, boo the loudest if it's required."

Chickadee put her fingertips under Luna's chin and pushed it up a bit. "And you must hold your head up and look haughty. That's my girl. Now I already read my poem. It was beautiful, don't be sad you missed it Dilly, I will read it to you privately later."

Dilly gave her a kiss, took her hand, and led her to the front row. Rebecca, Sarah, and Dan shifted to give them a seat. Rebecca whispered, "I'm glad you're back."

Dryden glanced down at Luna's hand entwined with Dilly's and humphed loudly.

Chickadee's friend Peter stood and read a poem next. Then another two people, and then Chickadee called Dilly to the stage.

Dilly said, "I have two. The first I've written, called, Simply Buzz.

Dilly beamed down at Chickadee and recited:

Flow and fly, righteously zooming, buzzing along with your . . .

It was a beautiful poem, about equal parts bees and Chickadee in a way that made Luna think, of course, the two were a perfect metaphor one for the other. Dilly had a way with words.

Chickadee had taken Dilly's seat and listened to the poem while holding Luna's hand. After it was over she whispered, "Told you it would be awesome."

Luna smiled but deep inside the tears were still coming. She kept watching this thinking — all borrowed, the house, the family, the life.

Dilly said, after the applause and whistles had died down, "As you have surmised, our beloved nephew Beckett couldn't be here today. He is off serving the Unified Mainland, against our enemies of men or elements — we aren't sure which, and he isn't saying because he doesn't want to worry us. But we worry anyway, don't we Chickie?"

"Yes, yes we do." Chickadee gave Luna's hand another pat.

Dilly continued, "We planned tonight hoping he would be here, so when he called earlier this week, devastating us with the news he wouldn't make it, he asked me to read something in his stead."

Dilly pulled an often-read, dogeared, paperback book from behind her back and thumbed through for a marked page. "My apologies, um, okay, here it is . . ." She folded the cover over. "It's a Calvin and Hobbes comic. One of Beckett's favorites. I know it's hard to see, but up here in this top corner, Hobbes, the tiger, is sitting in the wagon and asks, 'You really think this will work?'

"The boy, Calvin, is tied by a rope to the wagon and holding an umbrella. He says, 'Of course! Let's go!'

"The next square, Hobbes is headed downhill, and Calvin is flying. In the next square they narrowly miss this tree trunk." Dilly pointed at the following square. "Smash! Calvin has hit a tree limb.

"In the next square, Calvin is being dragged, bonk, bonk, bonk, down a hill."

Luna had a full cry happening, happiness and sadness rolled up into one. She was using a napkin to try to stanch the flow.

"Then Hobbes is rattling across a dock. Calvin is up-side down, bippity, bippity, bippity. Calvin yells, 'Look! I'm flying!' as the wagon dives into the pond. Hobbes flies through the air. Calvin is flying up near the clouds, and in the last square, Hobbes and Calvin are up to their mouths in the creek. Hobbes says, 'I had my eyes shut, how was it?' And Calvin says, 'Great! What a ride! Let's get some other kids and charge 'em!'"

Dilly beamed around the audience, then she cocked her head to the side and spoke to Luna directly. "I didn't understand why it was this comic, but Beckett told me you would know, Luna. And he said to tell you he loves you, and he'll be home soon."

Luna sobbed, nodded, and rolled up into Chickadee's arms. The audience clapped and whistled.

Dilly said, "That's our evening folks, please stay for refreshments, and, as always, the stage is open for your impromptu talents!" She met Chickadee and Luna on the front row and everyone hugged.

Rebecca said, "That Dryden girl left, right after Dilly read the comic."

"Good riddance," said Chickadee, "Not only did she toy with my Beckett's heart, but her family's been coming to our poetry slams for — how long Dilly?"

"It's been at least eight years."

"And in all that time have they ever read a poem? No, they have not. Not one. Participation is the entire point."

Dan held up his hands. "Hey now, we didn't read po-ems either!"

Chickadee threw an arm around his shoulder. "But see I like you, and it was your first one. Next time you'll participate." She sized him up. "I picture you as a bawdy limerick sort of guy."

He shook his head. "Nope, I save those for in private. In public I'm a gushy love poem kind of guy." He pulled Sarah close and kissed her on the cheek.

Rebecca said, "Oh my god, do you see what I have to live with? All this love — blech!"

Everyone was smiling. The warmth of the night, the crickets, the gathered people, the Calvin and Hobbes comic, Beckett telling her he loved her in front of everyone, the yummy food, it all colluded to bring Luna back to happy. A big happy. The kind of happy that made her want to cry.

Dilly put an arm around Luna and kissed her on the forehead. "You're past the halfway mark, now it's simply waiting for him to come home."

———————————

The end, but there's more to Luna's story...

Also by Diana Knightley

Leveling: Book One of Luna's Story

Under: Book Two of Luna's Story

Deep: Book Three of Luna's Story

Acknowledgments

A big thank you to my story editor, Isobel Dowdee, who found what was lacking and knew exactly how to tweak it and polish it and put a cherry on top. While steering clear of cliches. Your eye for detail is amazing.

A big thank you to Jessica Fox for dropping everything when I was ready for a beta-reader. Your speed and enthusiasm are super appreciated. And to Kristen Schoenmann De Haan who beta-read in the middle of completing her master's project. You're awesome. I hope you wowed them with your brilliance.

And to my family, Kevin, Isobel, Fiona, Gwynnie, and Ean, for listening to me talk vaguely about cliffhangers and watery worlds and what ifs that aren't grounded in reality, thank you. I couldn't do it without your help.

And thank you to my mother, Mary Jane Knight Cushman, she was a hopeful soul and taught me if the waters rise to grab a paddle.

And finally, to my father, Dave Cushman, who taught me that any story, like life, is better with a punchline.

About me, Diana Knightley

I live in Los Angeles where we have a lot of apocalyptic tendencies that we overcome by wishful thinking. Also great beaches. I maintain a lot of people in a small house, too many pets, and a to-do list that is longer than it should be, because my main rule is: Art, play, fun, before housework. My kids say I am a cool mom because I try to be kind. I'm married to a guy who is like a water god, he surfs, he paddle boards, he built a boat. I'm a huge fan.

I write about heroes and tragedies and magical whisperings and always forever happily ever afters. I love that scene where the two are desperate to be together but can't because of war or apocalyptic-stuff or (scientifically sound!) time-jumping and he is begging the universe with a plead in his heart and she is distraught (yet still strong) and somehow, through kisses and steamy more and hope and heaps and piles of true love, they manage to come out on the other side.

I like a man in a kilt, especially if he looks like a Hemsworth, doesn't matter, Liam or Chris.

My couples so far include Beckett and Luna (from the trilogy, Luna's Story). Who battle their fear to find each other during an apocalypse of rising waters. And, coming soon, Colin and Kaitlyn (from the series Kaitlyn and the Highlander). Who find themselves traveling through time and space to be together.

I write under two pen names, this one here, Diana Knightley, and another one, H. D. Knightley, where I write books for Young Adults. (They are still romantic and fun and sometimes steamy though, because love is grand at any age.)

Made in the USA
Lexington, KY
07 September 2019